MW01240686

The Children's

Home

The Children's

Home

By Mark Stattelman

Copyright © 2020 Mark Stattelman
All rights reserved.
ISBN-13:9798634084909

This is a work of fiction. Any similarities to any persons, living or dead, is purely coincidental.

Dedication:

To Genie.

Prologue

The young boy's foot slipped off the branch. He grabbed for the rope to steady himself. Dirt and a small piece of bark broke loose. He watched the bark falling to the ground. It took forever. He squeezed his eyes tightly shut, not wanting to see how far down it was. The girl standing on the branch next to him, looked over at him. The noose was already around her neck. She stood calmly, a serene look upon her face. She watched the tear roll down the boy's cheek. "Wait," the small boy mumbled, "Wait, I'm not ready." The boy's bottom lip quivered. His whole body, tiny as it was, shook and shivered. His little teeth chattered, creating an odd noise, a faint clattering sound. Another tear rolled down his cheek.

"Do it," said the voice. The noose was loose around the little boy's neck, but it had tightened some when his foot slipped. The voice was soft, firm, and commanding. It had been in the boy's head for at least a week now, just as it had with the rest of the children. It had been there before, but it had become more insistent as of late. "Do it." The voice had grown even softer now, yet still commanding. The little girl watched him. She watched the little boy get set. He settled and became calm. She smiled faintly, looking away from him. She looked straight ahead now. The voice spoke. The children dropped. Only two of them twitched and struggled, not strongly though. Mostly it had been smooth. The children hung in the morning dawn. One rope snapped, the windings of the coil unraveling. A small body fell. And then there were seven. Seven left hanging. . . dangling. There was a soft breeze. Hoarfrost rested on the branches upon which the children had been standing. Is that why the boy had slipped? A small bird alighted on the branch, on one of the outer, tiny fingers of it, just as the branch ceased its swaying. Another second and all was still, quiet. The small bird sang out into the dawn. It waited on an answer. None came. The bird flew away.

Chapter 1

I fancy Edwin MacCallum as a wee lad pouring over the stories of C. Auguste Dupin, the stories written by a Mr. E. A. Poe. Not everyone is familiar with the stories of course. Nor is everyone familiar with Mr. Edwin MacCallum. That's where I come in. And here is the tale.

I first came across the mystery of the Orphanage, or the Children's home, as it was called, when I worked as an intern at St. Catherine's in Washington. There was someone incarcerated there named–

well, let's just call her Alice. And she happened to have been, at one time, a resident of the Children's Home in a rural Virginia town. The town shall go nameless also, or I guess we could make up a name for it as a reference; We'll call it Riverton. Now, I don't know if there is such a town so named in Virginia, but I hope not.

In any case, I acquainted my friend, as I do consider him as such, with the story in a haphazard way one evening over dinner. He had been a college friend, or at least we would share a nod or so as we passed by one another. Then later on, well after the school years, I ran into him in the hospital in Philadelphia where I was working. He had broken an arm and was having it tended to at the time. Actually, he had broken the arm awhile back and it had since mended. I was, at this point, removing the plaster cast. We discussed old acquaintances, and hit the high points of our respective lives since college, etc. In any event, we agreed to meet for dinner that evening and I, for whatever the reason, over dinner, mentioned Alice. He was immediately interested in the tale and in finding out more about it.

After relaying the brief details as I knew them, he seemed to still have questions; and I must admit that I still had quite a few questions also. So, almost immediately, we set about acquiring all the newspaper clippings we could find from the time, regarding Alice and what had transpired in that small Virginia town. The case seemed far too incredible to be believed, which would normally have justified the incarceration of the person telling the story. But in this instance, we had the newspaper clippings to back up some of what had happened. The patient, for her part, had been far too traumatized to speak at all. Therefore, we decided to visit Alice at St. Catherine's now, to see if there had possibly been a change. And so that's how our story begins, more or less, and so it started with a simple train ride.

***

There was the steady clackity-clack of the wheels on the tracks, and the train's jolting back and forth. Overall, it was a beautiful fall day. I put down my newspaper and looked out the window. The leaves were beginning to turn to the usual fall colors. And I very soon found myself drifting into a meditative state. In the reflection of the glass I took note of my friend's countenance. He wasn't someone you would normally take note of. He was a decent dresser, not at all flashy. His suit was plain and worn just a little.

He was lanky in form, somewhat tall, but not con-
spicuously so. He had a distinctly receding hairline
and thinning hair all around, and a widow's peak.
His face was long and narrow, yet the jaw wasn't
necessarily of a strong set. Like I said, he wasn't
someone noticeable at first glance. He had a studi-
ous face, much like a youngish doctor would. He
had in fact studied to become a doctor, but for some
reason didn't go on to practice the profession. I had
heard that he had gotten high marks in school, and
was competent in the craft of medicine afterwards. I
had also heard that he had come from money, but to
look at him you wouldn't be aware of it. A young lady I knew said that he had courted a friend of hers,
Victoria I believe her name was. My friend said that
Victoria had said he knew very well how to treat a
lady; that he said and did all the proper things, but
that he seemed a little bored with it all. That is how
he appeared to me, to simply be bored with the
world and merely waiting on something to spark an
interest. He had an acute mind, but didn't necessarily spend a lot of time showing it off. However, it
seemed that when something struck a note with
him, as it were, or piqued his curiosity, he was like a

child; a child with a barely-contained, gushing sort of enthusiasm, a genuine interest.

"Do you think we're chasing a wild goose?" he asked, startling me out of my reverie.

"Dunno, maybe."

He paused and glanced out the window at the passing foliage while the train rattled and chugged along, and then looked back at me.

"Don't you find it at all curious that seven children were found hanging in the trees at sunup one morning, just out of the blue? That they hanged themselves?"

"Of cour--"

"That some supernatural being or force of nature persuaded them all to do it?"

I sat silent. He knew my thoughts on the matter. I wouldn't be here now, on the way to see Alice, had I truly believed that was all there was to it. With a slight shake of his head, he peered out the window again. The idea befuddled him, just as it had me so long ago. A sense of excitement rose up within me, just a tingling sensation easing slowly up my spine. We were going to find out. I saw the twitch of a smile on his lips as the train rattled on, moving ever closer to Washington, closer to young Alice.

***

It was a short carriage ride from the railroad station to the front gates of St. Catherine's. She stood just as I remembered her from several years before. The stone walls and tall iron gates. She reminded me of a castle belonging in a fairy tale. And it seemed one, a castle that is, that we entered now. I was determined to do things the right and proper way, even though we had no professional, or otherwise, need to be here. I had telegraphed ahead and hoped my current stature as a doctor, and my previous internship at St. C's would stand me in good stead. So up the steps we went and into the castle. The warden had left word that he regretted that he had to be off premises at the moment, but he would return as soon as possible. I was disappointed, of course, when I read the note, and looked around as to what to do now. MacCallum did not seem to mind in the least. I spied a young intern that I knew. Actually, I had known his older brother, but the young man had come to visit on occasion, and so I was familiar with him. He saw me and smiled, as did the orderly to whom he was speaking. The orderly grinned wide and waved, and I suddenly remembered an incident regarding this orderly, a minor problem, really, where I had stuck up for him and kept him out of the hot water he could have been in. The young intern came over to me with his hand extended. "Well, well," I prompted. "Following in your brother's footsteps?"

"And father's," he reminded me.

"Yes, of course." I had forgotten about the father.

"So, what brings you back?"

"Just a visit," I countered. "Though I had hoped to speak with the warden."

"Oh, well he's . . ." he looked around as though the warden might be just out of sight. "Gone. At least temporarily."

I raised the note the warden had left, to indicate that I was aware of the fact. I shrugged. What to do?

"Oh, this is a colleague of mine from Philadelphia, Dr. Edwin MacCallum."

"Pleased to meet you."

"Robert Fuller, I said.

"And you," MacCallum leaned in and the two men shook hands. He had tossed me a quizzical, but understanding look when I had used the term 'doctor' in connection with his name.

"I'm busy at the moment, but if you can give me about 30 minutes or so, I'll be able to escort you around."

A knowing smile crept across my face.

"Of course, I mean, you know your way. The place hasn't changed much, but . . ." He stammered blushingly for a second.

"Rules are rules, as they say. And no one can just wander around freely," I said.

"Right. But, hey, perhaps Henry wouldn't mind keeping you company until I return." He turned and motioned for the orderly. "Got a few minutes Henry?"

I for one knew that Henry had no more time to spare than young Robert, but he would gladly take it.

"Hey, Doc.," Henry said. "How've you been? Look atcha now, a real doctor."

"Henry. How are you?"

"I's fine, just fine, sir." He was grinning wide. "Things has changed some since you been gone. We got a man here now that thinks he's the good Lord Almighty. And he's a strange one, too."

"Henry, that's all fine, but I need to see Alice." I used her real name, of course, for Henry's sake.

"She ain't here no longer."

"Not here?"

"No, sir. When Ms. Ephram retired, she took her home with her."

"Took her home--"

"Yessir, you know how attached the girl became to her, and she took a special likin' to the girl. Guess somebody high up decided she wouldn't be no threat to nobody if'n she went home with Ms. Ephram."

"To live?"

"Yessir."

"Well, I guess she was no real threat then, now that I think about it. She was traumatized and we had to keep her heavily sedated. But--"

"Is her file still here?" MacCallum asked.

"Well, I s'pose it is . . ."

"Wait a minute," I said. "We can't just . . ."

"Why not? That's why we're here. Sure we can."

"But through the proper channels. . ."

"Do you think--?"

"The records are locked away . . . confidentially sealed."

"I know where the key is."

Both of us turned and looked at Henry. He was grinning widely.

"Do you honestly believe your young friend, Robert, stickler for rules as he is, is going to let us see her records?"

"Well, no, I guess not. But, the warden . . ."

"More likely an even bigger stickler when it comes to the rules." MacCallum turned to Henry. "What do you say, Henry, you up for it?" Henry was grinning impossibly ever wider now. I knew he was more than 'up for it.'

My collar grew tighter and tighter as I watched and waited. It is a wonder that I hadn't yet choked to death. I pulled out my kerchief and wiped my forehead for the twentieth time at least. Someone had to keep watch. Henry had known where the records were, as did I, but he knew where the keys were kept also. I did not. MacCallum could have kept watch, while I searched for the records, but he wouldn't have known how to head off our friend Robert. I just wished they would hurry up with it. I pulled my watch from my pocket and checked it again. It was already 5 minutes past time for Robert to return. If he didn't spot us where he had left us, he would hopefully assume that we had merely taken a stroll around the outer grounds.

And here Robert came, just as Henry and Mac-Callum rounded the corner. MacCallum shoved the file beneath his jacket and proceeded toward me. Robert had gotten sidetracked by an orderly who had a concern about a patient that refused to take his medication. Robert stopped to advise the intern on what to do, or perhaps he told him that he would himself come and resolve the issue. The second alternative would have been the best possible one for us. But we already had what we needed, apparently. I swallowed hard and wiped my brow once more as Robert approached. MacCallum and Henry were settled in beside me by then. Henry was grinning ear to ear, and was about to burst with excitement. The thrill of it all seemed almost more than he could handle. I felt the same, of course, though that feeling manifested itself in a much different manner in my case. I felt as though I might pass out. I'm not this skittish generally, but when it comes to my profession and the rules of it, I tend to side with the warden and young Robert.

"Well," said Robert, looking at MacCallum. "I hope you haven't allowed Dr. Benson here to get you into any mischief. I hear tell of many a tale from my brother that Dr. Benson was quite a prankster back during his time here." With that he gave me a light-hearted smile.

I could see that my friend MacCallum was grinning as wide as Henry now. I couldn't look directly at him, however. I was feeling ill enough as it was.

"Well, Robert, any chance we could--well, I best let Dr. Benson ask it, keep it official and all. . ." Mac-Callum looked at me. Robert looked at me. I could feel the perspiration popping out on my forehead, and I felt a bead of it run down my left temple.

"The records," prompted MacCallum.

I'm quite sure I turned whiter, paler by the second. "I, uh, well yes . . ."

Robert was looking back and forth, from Mac-Callum to myself. "Are you okay?" he asked me.

"I, ah, well, yes, it's just that I believe I may have caught a touch of something. Woke up feeling not quite myself this morning."

MacCallum raised an eyebrow at me. I could see it out of the corner of my eye.

"Would you like to sit down for a minute or two?" Robert asked, waving toward a bench in the distance.

"Oh, no, of course I'll be alright. We don't have that much time. We should be going anyway; We've wasted a good deal of your time already."

"Nonsense. There was something. . ."

"Oh, yes, um, there was a young lady, a young girl actually, residing here when I was here, her name was Alice, Alice Crenshaw. Any chance we could have a look at her records."

"Oh, no, I'm afraid not. You know the rules, of course . . ."

I nodded.

"Can't hurt to ask, now can it?" MacCallum chimed in. He glanced at me with glee.

"Oh, no, of course not. It's just that, well. . . perhaps the warden, when he returns . . ."

"Yes, yes. Of course. I understand completely." I pulled my watch out of my vest pocket and wiped my brow once again with my handkerchief. "And we've got to be going in any case," I said. "We have another engagement."

"Well then," Robert said, extending his hand to me, and then MacCallum. I just hoped he didn't notice the excess perspiration on my palm.

"Very nice to have met you," said MacCallum, extending his hand to Fuller. He was perfectly calm.

He then extended his hand to Henry. "And you, Henry. You were simply delightful company."

Robert seemed a little puzzled at the statement.

"Yes, Henry, It was a pleasure sharing stories from the past." I chimed in, trying to play my part.

Robert smiled then, his curiosity sated, I hoped. He looked at Henry with a slightly stern and official look.

"Well, I's best be gittin' on back to work now. Plenty to do, yessir. Nice seein' you again Doctor Benson. And nice meetin' you Mister MacCallum."

"Doctor," Robert chided.

"Oh, yes, certainly. Doctor, I's meant to say. Slipped my mind."

"No harm done, Henry. It often times slips mine also." With that, MacCallum gave me a wide grin.

Henry scurried on down the hall and disappeared around a corner. And we scurried on out the front and down the steps. Once back in the cab I nearly collapsed.

"Well done, Benson." MacCallum grinned at me, slapping me heartily on the back. He slapped the side of the cab to get the driver's attention, hollered up our next destination, and then pulled the file folder from beneath his jacket. "Now, let's see what we've got."

Turns out we had nothing. Unless we were interested in a Robert Greenbauer.

"Misfiled," I said.

"Or switched," responded MacCallum. "We'll know for sure after tonight."

I looked at him. My stomach started churning. The wheels of the cab rolled along the cobblestone road; The horse's hooves clopping along. The sun danced. There was a slight breeze blowing, moving the leaves of the trees as we passed along, the shadows playing on the ground. I felt faint then, as though I might pass out altogether.

"We'll just enlist Henry's assistance," stated Mac-Callum.

Chapter 2

After a short break for lunch at a restaurant off the boulevard, we started the leisurely pace out to where, if I remembered correctly, Ms. Ephram lived. I hoped she still resided at the same address.

"Okay, Benson, what do we know for sure about the case. Shall I call it that? Yes, that's what it is; that's what we shall call it. Take out the supernatural mumbo jumbo and what do we have? Eight children hanging from a tree with nooses around their necks. All dead, except one."

"Alice."

"Exactly. So what will she be able to tell us?"

It was a rhetorical question. He had no intention of my responding. This was his thinking process, at times. It was the after effects of the meal, and the pleasant weather on the drive out to Ms. Ephrams. The most obvious thing she could tell us is who it was strung them up like that, so cruelly, to dangle in the morning dawn. Though, of course, it didn't much matter the time of day; It was cruel nonetheless.

"As I recall the girl when she was first brought to St. C's, well, she wasn't very lucid, or responsive. We, the medical staff, all tried to induce her to speak. It was all to no avail. It was the trauma of the whole thing. She shut it out of her mind. Let's hope she has made some progress since. Perhaps she will be able to shed some light on things." Of course, I had my doubts. The girl was extremely traumatized at the time. She was battered and broken physically also, from where the noose had broken and she had fallen. Her head rested at an angle, from where her neck had been more or less broken. And to top it all off, branches had arrested her fall on the way down, which one would think would be a good thing. It was, in the sense of it saving her life; but one particular branch had taken out her eye and ripped a long runnel down her cheek, leaving a nasty scar that didn't want to heal. Poor girl. Thinking of the trauma, all she had been through, and the cruelty she must have had to suffer at the hands of other children, or their words at least. . . .One often wonders whether she might perhaps have been better off had the noose held tight.

"And it was a local priest who found her?"

"Yes, there is a monastery a short distance away. The priest was out at dawn looking for mushrooms. He is an avid collector, studies various species of fowl and fauna also. A father Andreas, if I remember correctly."

"And that fits with the news accounts?"

"I'm not sure exactly. I don't recall them mentioning that at the time. I believe it was kept hush-hush on account of fear for the girl's safety. But we knew. At least a couple of us on the medical staff, those of us handling her recovery and rehabilitation. "

"And so, of course, the killer, or killers have never been caught and brought to justice?"

Another rhetorical.

We rode quietly from then on, for another hour or so. I fell into a doze, my head nodding with each bump and jolt of the carriage. My dreams were haunted by the vision of children swinging, dangling and twisting in the morning dawn. That's an unfair characterization, in fact, my mind adding superfluous details. I would want to believe that the bodies hanged peacefully, rocking ever so gently, and that the children's souls were resting in a much more pleasant place entirely.

***

And so we came to the street, 18th and Vine, and pulled up at number 32, Ms. Ephram's residence. At least I hoped it still was the correct address. We alighted from the carriage and pulled open the gate. There was a woman just exiting the front door. She smiled briefly as she passed. We reached the door and knocked. It opened. "Yes?" said the woman standing before us. It wasn't Ms. Ephram.

"Oh," I said. "Sorry to bother you. I was looking for an old acquaintance, a Ms. Ephram." I had forgotten her first name. "I'm Dr. Benson. I used to work at St. Catherine's with Ms. Ephram. It's been quite a while, but--Oh, forgive my manners, this is Dr.

MacCallum. MacCallum's eyebrow rose again and a tiny smirk played about the edges of his mouth. I ignored it.

"Of course," she said. I'm Emily, Rita's, I mean, Ms. Ephram's niece."

We all stood smiling at one another for a couple of seconds. Emily turned and hollered Ms. Ephram's name into the room. "Couple of Doctors here to see you." She grinned at us. "I'm sure she'll be pleased."

Another woman appeared at the door. A face that seemed somewhat familiar, an older face, older than Emily's at least. It took her a moment or two. The puzzled look then turned into a smile. "Well, Dr. Benson," she said. "If it isn't you. . ." She seemed to have a little trouble finding the words.

"Yes, yes, Ms. Ephram, it's--"

"Oh, call me Rita, please."

I wasn't entirely comfortable doing so, and evaded it by introducing MacCallum.

"Pleased to meet you," she said. "Do come in, the both of you." She waved to Emily, who had apparently been on her way out and then stepped aside and ushered us into her home. Rita had been an attractive younger woman, and I believe she had been engaged to be married at one point, but all was called off for some reason or another. That's about all I knew about her. She was older now, and a spinster, though obviously not an elderly one. The somewhat vague impression I had of her took a more permanent form as she slipped into the mannerisms of a woman I now recognized. The term 're-tired' had been used, but obviously she was not elderly. I believe it had something to do with her father passing and leaving her a small bit of money. And though she had at least liked her job at St. Catherine's, and had a knack for it, good rapport with the patients, etc. It could be wearing. And now, if I remembered correctly, her father had been against her working there and being associated with the hospital. Perhaps there was something in the will that stipulated she quit. . . But that is complete speculation on my part.

And so we entered a small sitting room off to the left of the hall. "Would you care for anything?" she asked. "Any sort of refreshment."

"No, thank you Ms--Rita." I said.

"Sit, please, please." We all sat.

"Well now, to what do I owe the honor of your visit?"

At that point someone started into the room. A girl of about twelve or thirteen years of age. When she spotted us, she immediately turned and marched out. It was Alice. I had just caught a flash of her disfigurement. And the little girl she had been, the poor, sad, traumatized little girl popped ever so briefly into my mind.

"Alice, dear. . . come back, please. I'd like to introduce you to these gentlemen. One of them you might remember."

I could see her arm, her elbow and part of the forearm, and then the shoulder appeared and the elbow moved outward. She stood behind the wall, just at the corner, and seemed hesitant to enter the room. She had her back to the wall and it was her right arm I saw. I tried to remember which side the devastation was on. Her right, I believe. She had moved quickly out of the room, just in a flash, but I'm pretty sure that was the side. Yes, an image of her file popped into my mind and I saw it written, Right. I then realized she was fumbling for something. She slowly entered the room after affixing and adjusting an eye patch.

"Alice, plea--" Rita said, just as Alice entered. The girl entered slowly, and went over to where Ms.

27

Ephram sat. The woman rose and pulled another chair a bit closer and patted the seat. The young girl sat, hesitantly but obediently. She still seemed nervous.

Rita looked at us. "Alice tends to be a bit shy around visitors, most folks, actually. There's no reason for it really. She's a very beautiful young lady. Alice continued staring down at the floor. Her gaze never left it, in fact, even while Ms. Ephram introduced us. When my name was spoken, she seemed to want to bring her eyes, or rather, her eye, upward. She seemed to struggle to do so. A nervousness possessed her whole being, rising up suddenly out of the shyness. I felt as though she would jump up and dart from the room at any moment.

MacCallum sat quiet. He raised his head a second, as if intending to speak, but then seemed to decide to let me handle things for the moment. The girl was far too nervous as of yet for us to converse at all with her, let alone jumping right into questions concerning the traumatic event of her childhood.

"Alice," Ms. Ephram said. "Do you remember Dr. Benson?"

The girl again tried to pull her gaze upward, but to no avail.

28

"Hello Alice," I said in the friendliest manner I could muster. There was a hint of professionalism, or "doctorly voice" in it, but mostly a caring friendliness. She calmed for a minute, and then the nervousness was back. She began to tremble.

"Alice," MacCallum said.

"Gentlemen, I'm sorry, but . . ."

Alice jumped up and bolted from the room.

"Excuse me," said Ms. Ephram. She followed in the girl's footsteps. MacCallum and I were left sitting alone. I couldn't help thinking what a calamity of it all we had made. It had been a mistake to come. There is no way we would be able to question this girl. She had come a long way from the devastatingly traumatized little girl I remembered, but she still had a very long way to go. In the few minutes we had, sitting there, awaiting Ms. Ephram's return, I reflected on the little girl of five or six that I had seen at the time of her admittance. After her injuries had been administered to, and months and months after her painful healing process was under way, I would go in and sit with her. I would mostly just sit and be with her, to comfort her in some way. To observe, but also to comfort. She remained, at that time, in a state of shock, day upon day, week upon week, month upon month. The only person who could seem to get through was Ms. Ephram. With all of the others, all the doctors who tried to reach her, she remained impassive and immobile. She would sit and stare. Her eye, or socket was still bandaged. In fact, I was one of the ones early on taxed with changing the bandage, the cotton, bloody mess that it was. One day I started humming a tune, to myself really, a child's tune. Her good eye rose ever so slowly to look at me, just for a second. I pulled back and looked at her. The eye slowly went back down and she was settled back in her trance-like state. But just before I left her room, just as I was at the doorway, I heard something. She said something. "Tommy knows," she said. More of a mumble. I was afraid to speak. I wanted to ask about Tommy. "Who?" I finally said. And I could have sworn she spoke again, but I wasn't at all sure. "Tommy the mouse." I wasn't at all sure that it wasn't just in my mind. And, to be honest, with regard to just what Tommy the mouse knew, I eventually just brushed it aside. She never again came out of the trance in my presence. And I think in my mind I merely assumed she was talking about the tune I had been humming, that Tommy knew the song. It was a long, long time ago, and the mind plays fools of us all with regard to memory. But Alice . . .

Ms. Ephram returned at this point. We rose as she entered. She had a disturbed look on her face. We knew it was time to leave in any case. "Gentlemen," she said. "I–I don't know exactly what you wanted, but--"

"I'm sorry," I said. "We shouldn't have come without letting you know. . ."

"We had in fact come to speak with her; with Alice," said MacCallum.

"Well, I'm sorry you came all this way for nothing. But I would have warned you not to come in the first place. Alice has come a long way, a very long way. And I don't want to ever put her through any sort of agony with regard to her earlier life, to, to that . . . to what happened. Ever."

"I understand," I said. My friend nodded.

"I'm sorry," Ms. Ephram said as we reached the door. You saw how upset she became, just at the sight of you, Dr. Benson. I'm terribly sorry. And I hate to have to say this, but please don't ever come here again. Not to see Alice. Please, I beg this of you. I don't want to be rude, of course. But you understand." There was a definite pleading in her voice.

"We have every intention of heeding your wishes, Ms. Ephram. I'm sorry," I said. "Terribly sorry. Good day." I could sense MacCallum mustering a defense of our position. It was no more than a slight intake of air. I nudged him out quickly. Ms Ephram shut the door.

We went quietly. Once ensconced in the cab, and heading back, it was a long while before either of us spoke. "Well," started MacCallum, "There is only one thing left to do."

"Well, nothing," I said. We should let the past stay in the past. After seeing the girl, I felt abominable. I had no intention of going on with things. She was apparently doing well, or as best anyone could, under the circumstances. She was doing very well. And who were we, nosing around and upsetting the apple cart, hers or anyone else's? "We should cease and desist right here, right now."

"We must visit the scene of the crime," MacCallum said, as though I hadn't uttered a word. "Well, after we return the file tonight to the hospital."

I heaved a heavy sigh. I felt absolutely horrible. My stomach churned at the thought of going back to the hospital. Of course, we would have to return the file.

And there, the matter should be at an end. We must stop this madness . . . playing school boy detectives, really. It all seemed so absurd to me now.

***

I had been decidedly through with it all, finished. I was sure of it earlier in the day. I had to lie down when we reached the hotel. The whole day had been a strain. Alice's face, both the present one and from the past, kept floating before my eyes. The agony. I could feel her pain in a sense. I felt disgusted. Disgusted that we had been haughty enough to pursue things to the point of disturbing her. It had been an extremely callous thing to do. And then another feeling feathered around the edges. And this feeling then seeped in and rose up. This feeling was pure anger. The person who had hanged those children should be found and brought to justice. For Alice's sake. For all the children's sake. It was an abominable thing to have done. What that individual had done far outweighed us looking into the matter, disturbing the girl's peace. And so my thoughts shifted. Perhaps the several hours away from the visit to Ms. Ephram's, to Alice, the rest I had had, perhaps it had helped to sort things out a bit.

And so here we were, back at the hospital, attempting to put back the record we had pilfered earlier in the day. We shouldn't have done it, of course, but we had. And now it was time to put it back. We, the three of us, MacCallum, Henry, and myself, moved as stealthily as we could across the front grounds of the hospital. The castle-like structure loomed in the darkness. It was only another minute or so before we were at the entrance. Henry moved up the steps first and tried the door. Locked. He peered into the thick, mottled glass, and shook his head. He looked back at us. "Rufus was s'posed to be here to let us in." He shook his head again. We all waited. "Maybe round back," Henry said. Just as we started to turn and make our way around to the back, the door opened a crack. A young black man, far younger than Henry, had opened it. We slipped in. The young man was out of breath, and sleep rested around the corners of his eyes. Henry started to chide the boy, but then just shook his head. We moved off toward the records room as quickly as we could. I guess there really wasn't much reason for all three of us to go, but there had been no one to watch out for this time, and perhaps I could be of some help in finding Alice's record.

Henry unlocked the large wooden cabinet. He had handed me the file while he worked. I immediately found the proper place for Robert Greenbauer's file. I fully expected Alice's file to be inserted there. It wasn't. Another file was in that one's proper place, but it didn't belong there. "Henry?" I asked. "Who has the job of doing the filing these days?"

"Why, it's s'posed to be Miss. Ella's job, but she stays too busy. She gets me to do it, mostly, and I stick 'em right in."

"This is impossible," I said. "These files are all confused, all out of order, it's a wonder. . ." I had pulled a stack out and handed the lot of it to MacCallum to hold. He picked one off the stack and handed it to Henry.

"Here, Henry," he said. "I can't quite make out who this file belongs to" He had made a show of leaning forward and shifting the file in the lantern light. "I believe it says Andrews, or something, can you tell?"

Henry stood hesitant for a moment, and then leaned forward to look. "Yep," I believe you's right. Andrews."

"Henry," MacCallum said. "You have some trouble reading sometimes, don't you?"

Henry shuffled his feet a little and seemed to get nervous. "Well, yessir. Sometimes, I reckon I do. That's why's Rufus he'ps me out most times."

Rufus, of course, was the one who had let us in, and I suspect he wasn't a whole lot of help. I scoffed. I started to reorder the files, putting them in the proper places.

"That's okay, Henry," said MacCallum. "I tend to have a little trouble myself, as you just saw."

Henry raised his head up a little and glanced at MacCallum. He nodded and shuffled a little more, and then seemed to shrug the whole of it off.

I worked as quickly as I could, and had perhaps sixty percent of the filing done, when we heard footsteps coming down the hall. MacCallum was closest to the door. It had been standing open a crack. Henry extinguished the lamp. We stood in the dark and waited. The footsteps went on down the hall. When all was once again quiet, Henry re-lit the lamp.

It was impossible to lay the blame on Henry for the state of the files. It wasn't a case of just a few mis-read, or misplaced ones. The whole lot was out of order. I rearranged them all in the proper order as quickly as I could. "It's not here," I said. "Alice's file. It's gone, vanished." And then it hit me. The pa-

36

tients who are no longer in the hospital, their files get moved, down into the rat-infested basement. I mentioned this, a little perturbed that I hadn't thought of it sooner. I had no desire to go down there, but was saved in any case by MacCallum's observation.

"No need to bother any more about the file," he said. There is really nothing left to glean from it. You were her 'attending' physician, so to speak, when she was admitted."

"Well, among others."

"Yes, but you saw her, and read the file. You've seen the girl since. You can put together the pieces, should there be any to assemble a clear picture of how she got to where she is today. Not a lot of progress."

"I'd say there has been tremendous progress . . ."

"Yes, perhaps, but my point is you are aware of it. When we were wanting to look at the file this morning, we hadn't seen the girl. Now that we've seen Alice, with little or no result, there is nothing more that could be gleaned from the file itself."

"Yes, of course."

"And any of the particulars, at least of any importance, that were in the file, you can make us aware of, since you have seen it."

"Hmm." To a degree he was correct. There might have been an odd occurrence, or observation made and noted in the file between the time I had seen it and the time she was released into Ms. Ephram's care, however. And I started to protest on that point, but then decided we had no avenue really to follow if we found something. Perhaps later, I thought. It would be nice to find out when the girl came totally up out of her trance state. But, alas, we had been warned off from any attempt to find out. Anything.

And so with that, the wasted effort of searching for the file, we left the hospital. We said our good-byes to Henry. And I should note, he seemed a little sad to see us go. But in any case, the file we had gotten this morning was back in its proper place. I had noted that the folder had in fact been used for Alice, at one time or another. Her name had been crossed through with just a thin line, and Robert Greenbauer's name had been written beneath where hers had been. I suspected her file, all of the paperwork, doctor's notes and the like, was gathering dust and rat droppings in the basement. Perhaps some other night we could come and search for it. I was, in fact curious. It would have been nice, or perhaps revealing to have had a chat with Ms. Ephram about Alice, whether we had spoken to the girl or not. That prospect seemed not in the cards at the moment, or any time in the near future. I was sorry we had approached things as we did. Nothing could be done about it now, however. And so it would be off to Locust's grove, or, no, no, Riverton first thing in the morning.

Chapter 3

I t was another train ride through the ever-changing foliage of another beautiful fall day, each day growing a little crisper, cooler. And soon enough we were deposited at a small station in the town we were intending to visit in our search. It was the town that had suffered the tragedy of the hangings. I'm not sure that they ever quite recovered.

Our first intention was to stop by the local Gazette, the town's only newspaper. The place wasn't at all difficult to find. It was a two-man operation. A man by the name of Wiggs, owned the whole show, and ran the printing press. He did have a sidekick, a part time reporter, who set type and ran the press in Wiggs's absence. This man was named Jones, or "Jonesy," as he was referred to by the fellow citizenry.

Our reason for visiting here first was to compare notes, or to see if there were any articles we had missed regarding the "case," as MacCallum called it. The two were quite welcoming, and opened up the files to us. They cleared off a small desk and let us look through the back issues. Jonesy seemed to have an encyclopedic knowledge of the incident. And we asked him every question we could think to ask. Satisfied that we hadn't overlooked anything, we left. Later, on the street we ran into Jonesy again, and he offered to take us out to the orphanage, or "Children's Home," as it was called. It would have to be when he got off from work, around three in the afternoon. And so we went and acquired a room at the local Inn, and proceeded to go over our information.

"There's something that bothers me," said Mac-Callum.

"What's that?" I asked, eyeing him. "That the person who committed this foul and dastardly crime was never caught?"

"Well, yes, that, of course. But there is something else, something else entirely."

I waited for him to elaborate. He didn't.

"Shall we check in with the local constabulary?"

"Do you think they will be very welcoming?"

"No idea. But only one way to find out. Let's wait until Jonesy gives us the grand tour, however, before we poke our heads up."

"To be shot off, you mean?"

"One never knows."

Both of us had the sense that Jonesy would be more forthcoming prior to the authorities stepping in to quash our little investigative expedition. Neither of us had any supporting facts, nor any indication that the local sheriff would mind our nosing around, but we sensed that there could possibly be issues of which we were unaware. And most local authorities would probably be concerned with someone nosing about a case that, though not closed, was certainly years old, and long cold. And so we waited on our man Jonesy. Or at least we hoped he would be our man, our fount of information. One always can hope for some little tidbit, a tiny piece of the puzzle that hadn't been divulged before. We guessed that Jonesy would have just that. Or rather, we hoped as much.

It was three hours before Jonesy came calling, but he had a wagon with him and we headed out on the road. The Children's home was about three miles outside of town in a northeasterly direction. It was a pleasant ride out. I much enjoy the fall weather, if you haven't already guessed. And so we rode. And as we rode along, MacCallum peppered Jonesy with a few questions to get him started, and then he was off on his own for the better part of the journey.

The home had been started by two sisters well before the war had started. It had been called the Bedford School for girls. And this lasted for several years until the women, for whatever reason, decided to take in boys too, and gradually they started accepting any young child without parents. The two women needed funds, of course, to keep the place going, but apparently the ladies weren't the most talented fund-raisers, and they gradually became more and more dependent on the townsfolk. One of the sisters passed on and then the other tried her best to hold it all together, but the place became more and more dilapidated over time. The children became more and more rapscallion-like in nature. Supervision was sparse, or at times totally nonexistent. Eventually, the war came and the Union army commandeered the school for a short time, perhaps only weeks.

Here Jonesy paused for a minute, to move into lore, and away from any hard facts:

When the war was well-on, and nearing the end. There were soldiers roaming about the area, but not in groups. There were individuals, deserters, etc. And, in any case, rumor has it that the children, rascals that they had become, lured one in and knocked him on the head. They took whatever he had on him, anything of value, and then tied him up and began torturing him. Supposedly this went on for days, if not weeks, until the soldier died. At which point they buried him in the woods, and then waited on the next one to come along. But as you understand, this may just be a tale that's told and has gained traction over the years.

"And what of Ms., or Mrs. Bedford, the remaining sister?" I asked.

"Well, she had passed on at this point, and one of the inmates, or girls was old enough and took over the running of the place. She apparently didn't last. She met a man and then became in the way of child and left the school. For better pastures? Who knows? But the school, or orphanage, was without any supervision for a time.

A woman came in to take it over. She had come to town to teach in the local schoolhouse, but then she decided it best if she also took on the children at the orphanage. She eventually left the schoolhouse entirely. Some say she took to drink and used the children, hiring them out for jobs to help collect money for the place. This part is not entirely true, however, as far as I know. I tend to believe the story of the tortured soldier over this one, in fact." And with that, Jonesy ended his iteration of the school's lurid history. We had pulled up to the place, and gotten down from the wagon.

The building wasn't really fit for inhabitation. It had been closed down since that fateful morning years past. It still stands, but is in definite need of repairs.

THE CHILDREN'S HOME

We stood looking at a two-story wooden structure that the weather and time had worked on, and not in a positive way. The wood slats had turned gray and some had fallen off. There was a sign up on the upper level, just above where the roof of the lower level slanted out. The sign had been hanging just below, and between, two dormer windows. One end of the sign hung down. The Children's home, it read. Faded and fallen. One could almost picture what might have been at one time, or at least what might have been envisioned by some high-minded soul. One might imagine a colorful sign, and a brightly painted structure. One might imagine children's playful laughter springing forth, as the children themselves ran about and played out front of the school/home. One could even imagine a matronly female coming out on the front porch and calling the children in to dinner. They would all sit down at a long table, and there would be prayers and then an eruption of chatter, and a raucous, boisterous, splash of movement all round as they all partook of a hearty meal. And yes, I'm letting my imagination run here for just a moment. In any event, I needed to block out the horrible vision that was creeping around the edges of my mind at that moment. I

47

didn't look over to where the trees stood just to the left of the house, a bit in front. The scene that was captured in a photo the very morning of the hanging. I refused, just for the moment at least, to let that scene take over my mind. I preferred the happy one. However, looking straight ahead, and moving in that direction, toward the porch, there wasn't much to inspire any sense of happiness there either. Not really. My imagination disappeared and reality reared its head. Visitors? What's this?

I took a step up on the lower step leading up to the porch, and my foot crashed through the board. It's a wonder my ankle didn't twist in the process of smashing right through the rotten wood of the step.

"Careful there, brother," said Jonesy.

I pulled my leg out of the fractured hole while MacCallum supported my arm on one side and Jonesy attempted to reach out and help on the other. In another moment, without further mishap, we all three stood on the porch. We peered through the dirt-smeared windows, and then tried the door. It wasn't locked, but there was something blocking the way of the door opening. Someone had pushed a divan, or settee up against it from the inside. Between the three of us, we managed to open the door enough, that I could reach in and tilt the thing just enough so that we could work open the door a little more. And soon there was room enough for me to inch in and use my hips to work the divan in a little further; at which point we were all able to move in and give it a shove. One of the legs broke and the thing toppled as we pushed it off to the side. Once inside, we took a moment to stand and look around. There was a rocker across the room, sitting facing the door. It was off to the right. On the left, there wasn't much, except a few broken slats of wood and a small wooden crate that had been smashed. A small jar of murky liquid sat on the floor next to the crate. Overall, there wasn't anything of import in the front room. We wandered past a set of stairs and down a short hall. There was a room on the left. A single bed rested against the wall within. "That's where they found Ms. Mallory," said Jonesy. "She was fastened down good and tight to the bed, dead. Looked as though she had had an ordeal previous. It must have been a long and harrowing night for her."

"Cause of death?" asked MacCallum.

"Suspected poisoning, at least according to the Doctor."

"Suspected?"

"Oh, well, I reckon he was pretty definite about it. I guess the cynicism is on my part. There is so much of the events that seem up in the air about that morning. Too many questions. . ."

"Far too many," I chimed.

We stood for a few minutes longer looking at the bits of rope, still hanging from the bed. The rope had been cut, of course, to free the body of the woman. And a bit of sheet lay half spread out still, yellowed and deteriorated. There were rat droppings, and a bit of chewed debris resting in a pile on the sheet. A thin mattress showed beneath it all. The bed was iron, head and foot, a slightly rounded top, with bars in a vertical position. It would have been easy to tie someone to the bars at both ends and to the lower supporting frame. We left the room. The one across the way from it was completely empty of any furniture. There was simply a coat of dust, and more rat droppings. There were cobwebs stretched across the doorway. We left it undisturbed.

We went back out to the front, main room, and started up the stairs, making our way, stepping gingerly along the outer edges of the steps. The incident of the front steps was etched in all of our minds, of course. My ankle did feel somewhat sore.

And soon we were at the landing. Down another hall there were again, two rooms toward the back of the house on either side, and two rooms on the front side, a dormer window in each of the front rooms. There were beds in each room, similar beds to the one below, with the exception that no cut and frayed ropes hung from these frames. Nor were there any sheets or blankets. One of the beds had a mattress that had been pulled partly off the frame and an end of it rested on the floor. From the dust coating on the floor, no one had been upstairs for quite some time. There were more cobwebs. Candle sconces hung, one each, beside each door. These too, were covered with dust and cobwebs. There were candles of varying sizes, all used, some having burnt down more than others. The larger rooms had more beds, each lining the outer walls, heads against the walls and facing the hallway. And there were two beds along the inner wall of one room, end to end with sides pushed against the wall. Again, no ropes. With only one bed along the wall in the left side room. Other than what I have described, there wasn't much to see. My imagination returned once more. Again, it was easy for me to imagine a playful bunch of happy children, boisterous and laughing. Perhaps a pillow fight would start things off at bedtime and the woman from the room downstairs would holler up from the bottom of the stairs for the children to hush, to stop playing and settle down to sleep. It was very easy to imagine these things. And perhaps it was in order to keep the other vision from my mind, the one of the children hanging in the dawn.

And so back downstairs we went. And eventually we made our way out into the yard and around the back. There wasn't much to be seen there, however, except a broken-down wagon at the edge of the grown-up weeds. The brambles had overtaken the wagon and several flowers had even sprouted up between the spokes of one of the wheels. The wagon fell to one side, so there weren't a full set of wheels, and more likely a broken axle to boot. It was, as I said, covered in weeds and brambles, dying vines lay all across the top. Behind all this was nothing except woods.

Coming full circle around the house, moving around the left side, and moving toward the front, we came face to face with the large trees, one of which had supported the hanging children. I looked to the right and thought I saw a building, through another copse of trees and brambles, off in the distance. The trees were thin enough in that direction. And I could just make out a part of the structure. "The monastery?" I asked.

"Yep," answered our handy guide. "Sure is."

It was getting on late in the day, and Jonesy seemed itchy to get back into town. "We've seen all there is," said MacCallum. He gave me a glance. Jonesy seemed to agree, and so we climbed back on the wagon and headed into town. Jonesy dropped us at the Inn. We thanked him, waved good-bye and then headed to the nearest stable to hire a carriage for our own personal use. Once we had everything in order, we headed back out to the Children's Home, and then made our way to the monastery.

It was a small structure, but housed a large horde of monks it seemed. Not sure how many are housed in any one place, actually, but the place seemed to have a lot. The amazing thing was that it was extremely peaceful, quiet. It was unlike what I imagined the orphanage to be with regard to raucous behavior. Understandable, I guess. Monks, I imagine aren't the rowdiest of beings. We passed along a pathway that led to an entrance. When we knocked there was only silence for quite some time. Our knock seemed the loudest thing around, and I had the impression it reverberated in the air for a solid minute and a half. MacCallum had just raised his hand to rap again when a young man opened the door. My friend still had his hand raised; knuckles curled. The young man leaned back and away, as though he were going to have to dodge a punch. MacCallum brought his hand down. "Yes?" said the young man. "I'm brother Peter, how may I help you?"

"We would very much like to speak with Father Andreas, if we might."

"Oh," the young man said. "He is indisposed at the current time."

"Indisposed?"

"Yes, I'm sorry. He is ill, has been all afternoon."

"Oh, perhaps tomorrow then. Need we make an appointment?"

The young man, Peter, smiled politely. "No, no," he said. "It's quite alright. Pretty much any time during non-prayer hours is fine. He proceeded to lay out the schedule for us.

"Okay," said MacCallum, "we'll return tomorrow then."

We nodded and smiled. Peter smiled back at us and shut the door.

THE CHILDREN'S HOME

"Well," I said. "I guess that's that. Shall we head back to town then, get a bite?"

"In a bit," said MacCallum. "I'd like to take another run through the Children's Home."

"What could you possibly expect to find? We scoured the place earlier. Nothing much to see."

"Perhaps. But one never knows. Sometimes a second glance yields profitable results."

We headed to the Children's Home once again. It was as quiet and empty as before. The boisterous laughter I had imagined had been just that, my imaginings. It was every bit as quiet as the monastery had been a few moments earlier.

We went up the front stairs, avoiding the broken step, the jagged hole. "Must have actually been a nice place at one time," I said. MacCallum made no comment. I meant it too; it would have been a joy to see it full of little children. We entered the front door, not having to push the settee out of the way. Nothing stirred as we stood in the open front room with the broken crate and the jar of liquid, and the-- there was a sound, movement. The rocker rocked gently back and forth. We looked at each other, eyebrows raised. Supernatural happenings? MacCallum walked quickly over to the rocker. No one was sitting in it. He walked all the way around it. When he got around back of it the thing stopped, arrested in motion. The light was dim. It was late in the day, touching on evening, and evening shadows had moved into the room. It was getting on dark. MacCallum bent down, leaving his right foot placed firmly on the floor where it had been. He felt around. He pinched something with his fingers. "Benson, fetch the lantern, would you? It's still in the carriage. We should have brought it in."

"Gladly," I mumbled, mostly to myself. I didn't know what he had found, but I was still quite chilled at the movement of the rocker. I grabbed the lantern from the carriage, as asked, and hurried back in, almost stepping right into the hole on the step. Once I caught my balance, I took the time to light the lantern. I entered, the lantern's light spreading brightly about the room. Our shadows and the rocker's shadow were cast upon the far wall. MacCallum rose partially, and seemed to follow a line back from the chair. He was pulling the tiny, invisible line the whole while. He dropped to his knees about five feet behind the rocker.

"Bring the lantern closer," he said. Set it down here. I set it where he asked me to set it. He looked

up and smiled. "Mumbo jumbo," he said. He pointed to a small hole in the floor, about the size of a
nail head. "Look," he said, pointing to the hole.
"And this," he said. I picked up the lantern and saw
the broken thread in his hand. "And come here," he
said. We walked back to the rocker. He turned it on
its side. On both sides of the rocker, attached to
each runner, or whatever the bottom curved pieces
are called, there was a bent nail. "Wind a couple of
pieces of thread together, to make it just strong
enough. I don't imagine it would take too much in
the way of experimentation to make it work. Thread
the whole of it through each of the bent nails on the
bottom of the rocker and back to the tiny hole in the
floor. Tug on it just enough to set the rocker in motion, at just the opportune time, and then it either
breaks loose from the nails of its own accord, or one
can tug it hard enough to break it, pulling it on
down through the hole." He looked at me.

"Why, then that means . . ."

"Yes," he said, holding his finger to his lips to hush
me." He pointed to the floor. And then he began
pacing the room with the lantern, observing the
floor with intensity.

"Whew," I said. "It certainly gave me a fright to see that rocker start rocking." And after a few more seconds. "I'd feel more comfortable if we headed on back for now. Perhaps we can come back in the daylight." Nothing seemed disturbed. All was a layer of dust, undisturbed since earlier in the day. MacCallum moved methodically about the room. Then he went into the room with the bed, Ms. Mallory's bed. I followed quietly. The rope fragments still hung down. He peered beneath the bed and then looked up at me. He set the lantern down and pointed beneath the bed. I got down on hands and knees and looked. A trap door. And here the dust had been disturbed. MacCallum stood up, lifting the lantern.

"Well," he said. "Perhaps we should get on back, come back tomorrow in the daylight. I can't imagine we'll find anything here tonight." As he spoke, he motioned for me to stay sitting on the floor. He walked on out of the room and out into the front room. I heard him move loudly to the door, open it and go outside, taking the lantern with him.

I sat. I waited. I didn't have to wait long, however. There was a creaking sound as the trapdoor was pushed up. It came up just a little. I thought, as my eyes had adjusted to the darkness in the few moments since MacCallum had taken away the lantern, I saw a pair of eyes, just the whites, glistening in the darkness. I can't say how. I reached beneath the bed and slammed my hand down hard on the door. There was a frightened yelp, and a scuffling sound as someone fell. I jumped up and jerked the bed away from the wall, exposing the hole. I lifted the lid and saw only darkness.

Soon enough, MacCallum came back into the house with the lantern. We both stood looking down the hole. With the light it was easy to see that neither of us would be able to squeeze ourselves small enough to enter down into the hole from this end. We realized, however, that a child could come up through that hole and proceed to slip ropes across whoever might be peacefully sleeping on the bed that rested above.

As we approached the carriage, MacCallum filled me in on his doings while I waited poised over the hole. He said he had seen nothing out of the ordinary. He had turned out the lantern on reaching the carriage then, and waited for his eyes to adjust to the darkening night. The moon was on the rise. It didn't give off much light, but in any case, he rounded the house and darted this way and that across the grounds. I imagined him darting from tree to tree, peering out and around, hoping to catch someone on the run. Nothing. He had presumed them to have already gone, until he heard the commotion in the house. Still nothing. Or something, a child? A child playing pranks most likely. In any case, it was someone familiar enough with the grounds. There was nothing more we could do. We waited for a good while in the carriage before leaving. Nothing eventful happened. Apparently, that would be all the excitement we would have for one night. "We could always look around town in the morning and see who might be suffering from a severe headache," I joked. "I walloped whoever it was pretty good when I slammed the door back down. Just might have even caught a few fingers in the bargain. So we can keep a lookout for bandaged hands; at least one hand anyway."

"Hmm," smiled MacCallum in the moonlight. He shook the reins and got the horse moving. We headed back out to the main road leading toward town. I sat turned and looking back, surveying the area, looking for any signs of movement. Nothing.

***

THE CHILDREN'S HOME

In the morning, just before dawn, we made a fresh start for the Children's Home, hoping to scour the grounds and find the entrance to some secret tunnel, a passage that led beneath the house and exited up beneath Ms. Mallory's bed. We also hoped to make a trip to the monastery to speak to father Andreas. We saw him first thing, however, or at least we presumed it was him, and later found out that it in fact was. He was hanging in the dawn's early light, swinging gently with a noose around his neck, from one of the very same branches from which the children had been hanged. "I guess there's not much choice in the matter now," said MacCallum as we stood looking up at father Andreas. "We're going to have to deal with the local constabulary, like it or not."

Chapter 4

The Sheriff was a stout man, serious and capable. He was intelligent enough, but seemed a bit on the lazy side. He wanted things nice and tidy, but didn't much care for putting in the effort to make them so. He much preferred that old problems stay buried. Old cases, solved or not, held no interest for him. He would rather deal with the present. It was obvious at the current time that we were his most pressing problem. It didn't much matter that we were trying to get to the bottom of something that had happened years previous. He blamed us for stirring things up. He wanted to blame us for the hanging monk, but was smart enough to know he needed evidence. He didn't have any. He was sure, it became clear, that we had something to do with it, somehow. Our digging around had somehow, at least in his mind, prompted the monk's demise.

"Cut him down," he commanded his deputy. And then he turned to us and lifted his hat. It wasn't in greeting. He wiped his hand across his balding pate, and then brought it down to stroke his handlebar mustache. The ends of the thing weren't twirled upward, but hung straight down, hanging an inch or so below his jaw line. His face was red and puffy. He glanced our way and started to say something, but then realized that the Deputy had squirreled his way out on the limb and was sawing his way through the rope with his large knife. The body was about ready to drop. The Sheriff moved in beneath the dangling monk, who now twisted and turned just as the Sheriff grabbed his legs and the Deputy above sawed at the rope. The monk fell. The stout Sheriff held firm to him as he fell. The monk's dark cassock draped across the Sheriff's head. It covered his face and knocked his hat to the ground. This perturbed him all the more. I was quite sure he would rather be anywhere else on this fine morning.

The wiry Deputy had shimmied and then swung to the ground as quick and agile as a cat. He couldn't have been more than twenty-one or so, not long out of boyhood. He had a long narrow face, with man-like features, and thinning sand-colored hair. His chin had a growth of thin hairs, no more than pale strands. Upon his feet striking the ground he raced to the Sheriff's rescue. He at first couldn't decide whether to pick up the Sheriff's hat, or to help with the body. He made the wiser choice and helped with the heavier object. The two men carried the body to the newly arrived wagon. The wagon no more than stopped and the two men deposited the monk's body over the side. Our favorite newsman and tour guide, Jonesy, smiled from the driver's seat. He started to climb down, but the Sheriff shook his head. "You hurry and take this body on back to town." The Sheriff then swatted the horse's rear to set the beast in motion. One would assume that had there been a back way into town, the Sheriff would have told Jonesy to take it. The wagon circled around and was off toward town. The Sheriff walked back over and picked up his hat. He brushed it studiously for a minute, and then looked at the two of us. "Don't mean to be impolite, fellows, but I think it is time you leave this here town and head back to wherever you hail from. We don't need you here, poking around into the past and causing an uproar. The town is nice and peaceful, and we don't need any stirrings goin' on." He looked up at the hanging bit of rope as though studying its sawed-off end. The Deputy had come back to our little group, but stood three or four feet away. He was looking down and shuffling his feet a little in the dirt. He looked up and studied the Sheriff. He followed the gaze to the rope's end. And while the Sheriff gave his lecture, the Deputy decided to climb back up and saw off the rest of the rope. Before he was halfway to the tree, the Sheriff called him back. Apparently he thought it was best to let the elements work on the piece of rope, wear it down till it fell harmlessly to the ground.

By this time, the young monk who had answered the door yesterday, Peter, had made his way over to

our little band of merry limb-gazers and rope stud-
iers. He walked up gingerly and stood, looking meek
and harmless. He was a frail lad, with a shock of red
hair. A small cluster of freckles dusted each cheek,
just below inquisitive, pale blue eyes.

"Father Andreas hung himself," said the Sheriff. "Is
that clear to all of you?" He looked at us, waiting on
a nod of agreement. The Deputy was the only one
whose head bowed forward into a nod. The rest of
us stood in astonishment. Monk Peter looked ter-
ror-stricken, his mouth hanging open.

"But Sheriff," I started. "He couldn't have--"

"He did, hear? That's what happened! It should be
obvious to all. The man. . . and I know you didn't
know him, and weren't familiar with his ways, was
melancholy and suffered a sadness that wasn't obvious to all. And he dabbled in the effects of mushrooms . . . In any case, that's what happened. He
hanged himself. I'll hear no more about it." He
paused, looking sternly at us. He wiped his face
again after placing his hat on his head. Then he
puffed his cheeks and blew out air. He turned and
started back toward his horse. The Deputy started
after him. The Sheriff stopped after a few steps, as
though he was going to lecture us on something. But

all he did was tell the Deputy that perhaps it was best to cut the rope off the limb after all. He didn't add this, but one could easily follow his thinking: Best not leave any sort of evidence of any wrongdoing. Best to keep rumors at bay and keep the town peaceful and happy. It had been a very traumatic event when the initial incident occurred. No point in stirring things up again. He glanced at us and then moved again to his horse. The Deputy followed quickly behind, but only after securing the release of the rope from the branch. The three of us watched the two men leave, and then looked at each other

"But he couldn't have . . ." said the young monk. He was staring up at the empty branch. MacCallum and I agreed with his statement. We were all aware that it was considered a mortal sin to commit suicide, at least by Catholics. The three of us continued to stare upward, the sun glistening behind the branch now. The sky was a cloudless blue. Hoarfrost still rested on the branches and leaves, with the exception of the one the Deputy had disturbed, but it was dissipating quickly in the sunlight.

"How devout was Father Andreas?" asked Mac-Callum.

The young monk brought his gaze from the limb, looking directly at my friend. He appeared to be almost offended by the question. "Extremely," he said.

MacCallum nodded.

There was a pause as the monk looked once again up at the limb. "He was an extremely devout man," he said. It was almost a muttering to himself, as though he couldn't comprehend anyone even asking the question. He thought it through for a second, gave it due consideration, but had no reason to change his answer. That settled it for all of us; Murder, plain and simple.

Chapter 5

"So James Carroll wasn't the sheriff at the time of the hanging of the children?" MacCallum asked Jonesy. We were standing in the newspaper office. Jonesy had deposited the monk's body at the undertaker's and was now standing at the press. He was ensconced in a printer's apron, and had the visor atop his head. He had been setting type when we interrupted.

"Why, no sir," he responded. "Rupert Rowlands was sheriff then."

"But the articles have Mr. Carroll as sheriff."

"Yes, sir, but . . . those articles were written later, after he took over. . ." Jonesy lifted the visor and sighed. "See, Jim, he was Deputy then. Sheriff Rowlands passed away shortly after the hangings.

"And that's when Deputy Carroll took over."

"Well, yes, that's exactly right."

"What did Sheriff Rowlands die from?" I interposed. Perhaps it was simple curiosity as a doctor.

"Heart attack. He passed within two weeks or so of the hangings."

"I see," said MacCallum.

I nodded.

I heaved my own sigh. "Well, not much more we can do about figuring out any of it."

Jonesy looked puzzled.

"Sheriff ordered us out of town. Seems he prefers the peace and quiet that was here before we arrived and started 'nosing around'."

Jonesy tried to suppress a grin. He shook his head. "Well, he can't blame you for Father Andreas' hanging. . ."

"Why not?" asked MacCallum.

"He as much as laid the matter on us already. Had there been any supporting evidence, we would be in cuffs now."

Jonesy shook his head and frowned. Then an idea struck him. "You know," he said. "I believe I can help there. I have to do it on the sly, however. Because Wiggs is having lunch with the sheriff now. The two of them are pretty tight."

"What do you have in mind?" I asked.

"Leave that to me," he said. Then he thought about it a second and decided that I might in fact, be of some assistance. "Mrs. Rowlands," he said. "She still has a lot of pull around town. Most of the townsfolk still respect her, and sheriff Rowlands was sheriff for quite a long time. Most everyone here looked up to him."

This left the question of the current sheriff, hanging in the air. "Oh," said Jonesy. "They respect him too, but in a much different way, I guess."

"So how will she help, Mrs. Rowlands?"

"Well, she always liked me well enough. And it was sad that the case was never solved. I'm sure, if I explain things . . . and with your help, we might just be able to persuade her that it would be good to solve the case, her husband's last. . ."

MacCallum nodded and agreed it might work. I wasn't quite convinced, as yet. We had muddled things a bit. Not with Father Andreas. We had nothing to do with that, of course. But I did think of Alice, and how we had botched things with her. But then the anger started to rise up again. Someone should have to pay for all of those children, and for Alice.

"I'll do it," I said flatly.

"Great," said Jonesy. "Like I said, it has to be on the sly. I can't let Wiggs know that that's where I'm off to, but as soon as I can, after I get finished here, and once he's back, I'll come get you then."

"Jonesy," said MacCallum. Have we seen everything there is to see regarding the case? All the articles?"

"Well, yes," he said. "All the articles, sure. Everything." He wiped his hands slowly on his apron, thinking, and then scratched his head just behind his ear. He lifted the visor and placed it back. He slowly grinned. "There is one more thing. I plumb forgot about it. I'll have to dig around a little to find it. It isn't an article, but . . ." He grinned wide now. "I forgot completely that I never returned it. I don't even think it was ever missed, as the case was abandoned." He wiped his hands again, and went to a door. We followed. The door opened onto a small room, a storage room of sorts. There were cleaning supplies, and shelves of wooden crates, old issues of the newspaper, and files. He dug around for a minute. Pulled a box off an upper shelf and looked through it. He pushed it back, frowning. Then he pulled another box down and went through it. Then he went for a third box. And there it was. He pulled out what appeared to be a bound volume, a ledger of sorts. He grinned and handed it to MacCallum. "The record book from the children's home. Lists all the children over the years who stayed there, what date they checked in, when they checked out. Even has some medical notations about when any of the children were ill. . . I can't believe I didn't think of it sooner." And that's when we heard the door of the shop open. Wiggs.

  MacCallum shoved the book under his coat. I wasn't sure why at first, as Wiggs had been helpful enough regarding any articles on the incident. But, that had been prior to his having lunch with an unhappy sheriff, his friend.

"Gentlemen." He tipped his hat. He eyed Jonesy a little suspiciously for a second. And then he started to say something, but stopped himself.

"Thanks for returning the articles," said Jonesy. This statement eased the tight look on Wiggs' face.

Wiggs pulled out his watch and looked at it. "And we've got to finish the typesetting. We've got a paper to run." He looked at us. "Good day, gentlemen." Jonesy had already moved over and was back at work. He simply smiled and waved at us and then ducked his head quickly, his attention absorbed by the type. He had a smudge of ink above his eyebrow that I hadn't noticed previously. His brow was creased in concentration.

Back out on the street and heading to our hotel we were. "I would venture to guess Wiggs was about to mention the sheriff having asked us to leave," I said.

"Yes, I'm quite sure of it." Both of us were glad of Jonesy stepping in and covering us. He had turned out to be our man after all.

As we walked, I spied the sheriff across the street. He had stopped, just as I glanced, and I was sure he was going to come across and reiterate his earlier message. Instead, he wiped his hand down his outward puffed cheeks and downward across his lengthy mustache. His hat was held in his other hand. He turned it. Still standing, still watching, he was reiterating the message without actually uttering a word, I realized. The two of us continued on our way, not quite hurrying, but not wanting to rile the sheriff needlessly. After Jonesy and I spoke to Mrs. Rowlands, things might be different, but for now, we should probably lay somewhat low. Not having met the respectable Mrs. Rowlands yet, I still had some doubts as to our prospects. The sheriff was wanting us gone, and the sooner the better. He had a town to keep quiet and peaceful.

***

Once up in our room, I lifted the edge of the curtain and peered out the window. I looked at my watch, wondering if the sheriff would still be standing across the street and watching our hotel when Jonesy came by for us. Or me. I was under the impression that it would just be me and Jonesy making the trip out to the widow's home. MacCallum had already pulled the ledger from beneath his coat, and was perusing it. And just as I was dropping the edge of the curtain back into place, I saw the deputy come out of the telegraph office, which was right across from the hotel. I figured the watch was being relieved. It was the deputy's turn. They were going to make sure we left after all. "I wonder if there is a back way into the hotel for Jonesy to take?"

"He's a resourceful fellow," said MacCallum. "He'll figure something--"

There was a knock on the door to the room just then. I looked at my watch again. Still too early for our man. I lifted the curtain back a fraction. Both men were still standing across the street. The knock sounded again, a soft but solid knock. I took a step, but MacCallum was already at the door and opening it. I couldn't see who it was from where I stood. The door blocked my view. "Come on in," said Mac-Callum. Turned out it was Peter, the young monk. He was clearly nervous and agitated about something. His face was contorted in the anguish of indecision. Freckles were astir.

"Sit, please," said MacCallum, indicating one of the two chairs. He took the other. I perched on the edge of the bed. The young man sat, but not comfortably. "What can we do for you?"

Peter's face contorted and formed into various shapes of uncertainty. I wondered how long he would last at the monastery. Or perhaps it would be the best place for him. It would at least shelter him

78

from the terrors of the outside world, until he could mature and gain some steadiness. Though, I thought, it hadn't sheltered him today. Father Andreas' death was front and center in his world. And that, obviously was what he had come to talk about. He pulled a letter from beneath his cassock and handed it to MacCallum.

MacCallum studied it for a minute or so and then handed it to me.

"I found it under my pillow, after I returned to the monastery, after . . . after. . . I, I, don't know when he could have placed it there. It must have been while I was at morning-prayer. Sometimes he goes—went . . . early, and then would go out in the woods to look for mushrooms. I think mostly he just . . . just enjoyed the early morning walks." A tear escaped from the corner of one eye, and then more followed, from both. I glanced at MacCallum and he at me. Both of us were at a loss as to what to do to comfort him. While waiting for him to pull himself together, I cleared my throat and read the letter. Not aloud, actually, but this is what it said:

Peter, should I not return from my walk this morning, there is something I'll need you to do. I want you to find my private diary and hang onto it. Remove the third brick from the right, counting outward from the head of my bed. It will be loose. You can jiggle it out easy enough. My journal will be within. You will best be in a position to figure out what to properly do with it. You can turn it over to the authorities. If you need guidance, and I'm guessing you probably will, place your trust in the Lord. However, should you feel you need more earthly assistance, then speak to Fr. Bartholomew. Be brave, son. My soul will be looked after.

I looked up from my reading. MacCallum was watching the boy. Peter had gathered himself, at least somewhat, at this point. "Have you spoken to Father Bartholomew?" asked MacCallum.

"No."

MacCallum nodded. "The journal, have you retrieved it yet?" There was a long silence. I'm quite sure neither of us expected young Peter to have gone after it. He needed time. I had time then to conjure up an image of the terrified young man, or boy, going into the deceased monk's quarters and searching for the journal. I couldn't see him doing it, not alone. I had visions of him trembling, pulling out the loose brick, his fragile, shaking hand banging the brick from side to side, edges of the brick crumbling and falling down the front of his dark robe and then onto the ground. I imagined the silence, and Father Andreas' spirit standing just behind him. And should that spirit tap him on the shoulder, or speak . . .

"Yes," he said. And, from beneath his cassock, he pulled a curled mass of parchment, a sort of book, pages crudely sewn together along one edge. The cloth binding that formed the sides was torn and loose. The whole of it was yellowed and starting to decay. Father Andreas's journal had spent years, apparently, tucked away in the dark and musty crevice, the hidey-hole behind the brick.

MacCallum took gingerly hold of the book as young Peter handed it to him. He opened it with care, and then flipped through it as roughly as he dared. He looked at Peter. "And so you would like us to hand it over to the Sheriff for you?"

A sudden alarm rose up in Peter's face, his eyes wide. He stammered for a minute. "Why, no," he said. "I thought, I mean . . . won't you look into the matter?"

"But Father Andreas, at least according to the letter, wants you to turn it over to the authorities."

"Well, yes, but . . . But he also says to use my judgment and I don't think the sheriff cares in the least about figuring out how Father Andreas died. I mean, who killed him, of course, not the manner of his death. You heard the sheriff as much as say he had no intention of looking for anyone."

"And what makes you think we can do anything?"

"Well, you're looking into the other . . . the hanging of the children."

"What makes you think so? We never even got the chance to speak to Father Andreas. And, besides we've been asked to stop looking into anything, to stop stirring up trouble."

"Why, practically the whole town knows you are looking into the children's hanging. It was very obvious from the first, from the minute you showed up."

MacCallum glanced at me, before responding. "How do they know?"

"It is a very small community, and anyone, any stranger who shows up, is usually only here to ask about the hangings. It has been that way from the beginning, from when it happened."

"And you were here then?"

"Well, no, I've only been here for a little better than a year, but I've heard the tales."

"I see," said MacCallum. He sighed, and gave it some thought. "Well, we'll look this over, and think about things overnight. We will let you know in the morning. Does that suit you?"

"Well, I guess it's fair enough. But--"

He rose slowly from the chair, not sure whether to head to the door, or drop to his knees and beg. He took several steps toward the door.

"Is this all?" MacCallum held up the journal.

A look of panic spread over Peter's face. He was startled. "Yes, ye–s, of course. What do you mean?"

"Just wondering if this was everything?"

"Yes."

"Well, then." MacCallum smiled at the young man and rose to see him out.

I got up and went to the window. The sheriff and deputy were no longer in view across the street.

"Why were you so hard on the boy?"

"Look for yourself." He motioned to the journal.

"What do you mean?"

"It's worthless to us," he said. "Unless there is something that can help us that hasn't been ripped

83

out." He opened a small case and tossed a magnifying glass onto the bed beside the book. I picked the glass up and thumbed through the book, not sure what I was to look at, exactly. "You'll notice, some pages are ripped out, right out of the mid-section."

"Yes, but it could have been Father Andreas who ripped them out. After all, he could have torn out a page from this very book to write the note to young Peter, instructions on finding the diary."

"He did, apparently. He tore that page or two from the back. And there are other sections, where pages have been torn out. But if you look closely at the bits that are left, you will see that the pages that had been torn out previous, left a ridge, just like the newer sections. However, if you look closely, you'll notice that the older sections are yellowed and have the brownish, mottling similar to the pages. The fresher ridges, where pages have been ripped out recently have a lighter edge. And, if you'll note, the torn pages are from the inner section, which isn't as loose as the outer sections. The book is falling apart, but the binding toward the center is still holding together. I suppose there could be more pages missing from the back, or front of the book."

I held the magnifier over the ripped edges. I could see what he was referring to, but it still could have been Father Andreas who had ripped them out. And I said as much.

"Nonsense," said MacCallum. "The boy is looking after the older man's reputation. The problem is that we need the whole to glean what all of it means. Perhaps the purloined pages mean nothing at all, and once we have a look at them, we'll be able to tell. There must be something relevant in the book, otherwise the good Father would not have left the instructions for Peter."

"And how do you propose to have a look at the 'missing' pages."

"You saw him. The young man's guilt will eat away at him until he turns them over to us. . ."

"And you were trying to help things along a bit. Hmm. I see."

"He'll be back to hand them over. He probably won't sleep much tonight. I suspect we'll have the rest of the pages in the morning."

We had just started to look over the ledger when a knock sounded on the door. I looked at MacCallum. He shook his head. To early yet for the boy's guilt to have worked its full measure. I opened the door and Jonesy stood smiling at me.

"Well," I said. "Early."

"Yessir," he said. "Finished in record time. And I told Wiggs I had an errand to attend to."

I grinned and grabbed my hat. "You coming?" I asked MacCallum. He was bent over the ledger, studying it.

"Hm? Oh, no. Go ahead. The pleas to the sheriff's widow might not work. I want to look over as much as possible in the meantime. We'll need to glean as much as we can, and see what it yields . . ."

I nodded in agreement. Jonesy and I left. I hoped the errand would be successful. And I also hoped that there would be something to be learned from the ledger, as well as the monk's journal, missing pages notwithstanding.

On the way to the widow Rowland's place, I questioned Jonesy about the orphanage's ledger. I hadn't yet had much of an opportunity to observe it. I figured he had been through it pretty thoroughly at least once or twice. Perhaps not recently.

"Well," he began. "I had studied it close enough soon after the incident. But, to be honest, it has been a couple of years since I looked through it. I had actually forgotten about it till this afternoon. What do you want to know, exactly?"

"I don't know. For starters, I guess you can elaborate on some of the children staying there. . . Did you know all of them? All of the hanged ones?"

"No. Some, I did. But not all. I know the names, of course, of the hanged ones, the poor little devils."

I preferred to think of them as angels, myself. I'm sure he didn't mean it as such . . .

"Let's see, hmm: There was Quincy Bode, and little Charlie Furman, then Katie Tinsdale, Marjorie Thune, Billy Herron, Becky Anders, Alice Crenshaw, Amy Johnson, and Tommy Mifflin, and well . . . others, before and after. And Tommy Mifflin didn't hang, of course. He wasn't there that morning."

"Ah, so one escaped. Besides Alice, I mean."

"Well, don't know if I'd call it an escape, exactly. He would come and go. His older brother had stayed there a few years earlier, but then became old enough that he was able to get out on his own. And sometimes the younger brother, Tommy, would stay with him. Now Tommy works at the stable in town, sleeps there as well, most nights. The nights he's not there, I would imagine he spends them with Daniel."

"Daniel?"

"Yes, but you already met him."

"Hmm? Don't recall him. We haven't really met anyone since we've been here, outside of you, Wiggs, and the young monk, Peter, and . . ."

"The Sheriff and the Deputy."

"Well, yes, but--"

"Daniel is the deputy."

"Oh, I see."

"And you rented the carriage from the hostelry, so you probably met Tommy. He's the skinny kid." He grinned. "The one with the shiner."

"What?"

"Well, not so much a shiner as a lump on the fore-head. Horse kicked him the other day."

"Hmm, did it now?" I, of course, got to wondering about Tommy now. "Haven't actually seen him," I said. "An older gentleman rented us the carriage. Gruff sort of fellow."

"Oh, yes. Mr. Farrow. He's not as mean as he tries to make out. And, he took Tommy in a few years back, to help out. Not the best help, I would imag-ine. But I guess he does all right."

Hm, I thought. When he's not off playing pranks on newcomers.

THE CHILDREN'S HOME

Another couple of minutes and we were at the widow's place. Perhaps once I had a chance to look over the ledger, I could ask more in-depth questions about each and every child. As he had stated, he didn't know them all. But maybe he could give some more information, a little more detail. I began to wonder if I was more interested in the information so I could fill in the images of the live children that I had played out in my mind. I would love to actually see them running about and laughing, etc. That, of course was an impossibility. But the mind and heart wished to get a glimpse. Perhaps I needed something to override the image of them hanging in the dawn, their little necks broken . . .

Mrs. Rowlands was a kindly enough woman. She seemed to have aged well. She had a full figure, a matronly sort, friendly. She smiled, but the creases around her eyes and mouth bespoke of sadness. Perhaps I'm reading too much into her appearance. She was friendly and warm. However, when it came to helping us, I wasn't sure where she stood. At first, she didn't seem too inclined to help. She even winced a little when Jonesy suggested she might could help us convince the current sheriff. "I don't know," she said after a few seconds thought. "I just don't know. Seems like too much time has passed now to really accomplish anything in the matter. It is a shame, of course. . ."

We dropped the matter for half an hour or so, as she showed us around the place. It was quite a spread. Beautiful country. She had a few head of cattle, and some chickens, a couple of goats. A mutt of sorts had come sniffing around us at first, and gave a growl or two at me, but then settled down. And so we wandered and spoke of other things. I got the sense she was weighing it out. By the end of our visit, she said she would think about it overnight. She made a comment indicating that it would be nice, at least for her husband's sake if something got solved, or figured out. It would be ideal, of course, if someone could be brought to justice. She didn't, at least from the impression I got, have too much faith in sheriff Carroll's help. Jonesy made a final plea to her, mentioning how helpful it would be; and of course, I echoed his sentiments. Then we covered the 'nice to have met yous' and, were off again toward town.

When we got back to town it was growing dark. We went up to the room and MacCallum had lit a lamp. He had dismantled the whole of Father Andreas's journal. "Young Peter is going to have a stroke," I said. MacCallum chuckled. He had all of it laid out upon the bed. He was placing it page by page, one atop the other, and actually beginning to sew it all back together.

"Nonsense," he said. "I'll have it all back together before morning. And in much better shape than it had ever been." He had apparently gone and purchased some heavier thread, or fishing line, along with a large needle. He had also made another purchase, I noticed. Lying across the bed was a walking stick. At least I didn't remember him having it in his possession on the way down. I picked it up and inspected it. It had a skull's head at the handle end of it that appeared to be formed of silver, and the other end had a tip of metal. It was quite intricate in design, professionally made.

"Oh, yes. When I wandered out to look for the line and needle, I happened upon an old black gentleman who was in possession of it. I had an uncle who once owned one very similar to it. The man said he had purchased it from a gentleman passing through town several years back. It cost me a great deal of effort, and a pretty penny to get the black man to part with it. But in the end, there's no accounting for a man's wants. Seems cash will eventually persuade most any man to part with most anything. And watch this," he said. He touched the head of the cane, his finger alighting on a hidden catch of sorts, and the head pulled up out of the cane, a long thin blade following it out. It wasn't quite a full-length sword, more like a rapier. "I'm not sure the man I purchased it from was even aware that it was a weapon. Though, a simple cane, or walking stick could always be used as such. But I believe the gentleman simply used it as a walking stick. Had he known about the sword I would imagine he would have driven an even harder bargain." With that, MacCallum began to move about the room, thrusting and parrying with an imaginary foe. He was quite agile in his movements. I smirked at Jonesy, and he simply couldn't suppress a grin.

  "Oh, by the way, I believe our prankster from our visit to the children's home is the local stable hand. According to the man I purchased the stick from, the boy supposedly got kicked by a horse. But I'm quite sure it was the trap door that caught him. From the description I got of the boy, he is small and wiry enough to have fit through the door and into the tunnel." MacCallum slid the blade back into its holder and tossed it on the bed. He sat back down and began sewing up the journal.

Jonesy and I sat in the two chairs. I flipped through the ledger, and we proceeded to discuss it. I would read off a name, and he would, to the best of his knowledge, provide me with information on the child. The book listed dates each child was taken in, and then the date each child would leave for good. Of course, sadly, the hanging children's departure dates were left blank. There were initials in the back, next to notations on the children's health. A doctor would come to visit periodically and observe each child's health; and if a child was unwell, he would attend to the illness. He would leave a line or two, notating the illness, what he had done in attempts to relieve it, etc. A little further back in the book, or rather in the front section, which went back in time, there was listed the children who had been there much earlier than the children who died so horridly that final day. A few years back, I saw the listing for Daniel Mifflin, his entrance, and then his departure. As I was flipping through the book, I noticed another entry. This one in particular, caught my eye. Tommy Mouse! Really, it was Tommy Muse, but in between the letter 'M' and the letter 'u' someone had squeezed in the letter 'o.' It had been written in pencil, and then afterwards, someone had tried to rub it out. It was still visible, just barely. I'm guessing, had Alice not muttered "Tommy the Mouse knows," that day years ago, I wouldn't have noticed anything unusual in the book. And had I not thought of that day, on the visit to see Alice, it still might not have registered now. I pointed it out to Jonesy. He smiled. "Yes," he said. "Tommy the mouse was legendary with the children. He fits in with the tale of the Yankee soldier that got tortured and killed. A boy, little Tommy, wouldn't go along with the plan. At least according to the tale. And that night, several of the children, fearing that little Tommy Mouse would turn them in, strangled, or smothered him in his sleep. I flipped through the book, looking for any sign that Tommy the Mouse had departed the home in the usual manner. I couldn't find it. Jonesy continued, "The children, up until the end, swore they could still see little Tommy roaming about the place. Some would even say he spoke to them."

I flipped back through the book, searching for the dates that Alice was at the home. She was there much later than Tommy had been. She didn't even enter the home until several years after the war. I shrugged. Children have an amazing imagination, and once a tale gets started, well, there isn't any stopping where it might lead. As time passes, the tale most often grows in stature.

"There," MacCallum said. "Better than new!"

"Peter will be offended, I'm sure, that you had the audacity to fiddle with Father Andreas's handiwork. I'll be interested in seeing how he takes the newness of the journal."

"And I'll be just as interested in seeing the pages he has ripped out. When he hands them to us."

"You're still thinking he will?" I asked. "Or that he actually has them."

"Of course. He'll come knocking and confess all. Though I'm not sure the pages will actually be of any help to us." He looked at me in all seriousness. And I laughed heartily.

"This, however," said MacCallum, pulling out a small bit of folded up paper and tossing it to me. "It is quite interesting. I found it tucked into the back binding. I noted the threads there were loose, but were *neatly* loose. The other parts of the binding that the threads had pulled loose from, well they were more haphazard in nature. I pulled the neater threads out to look, and found a small pocket behind the binding."

I read the note in astonishment:

The girl is still traumatized. She isn't speaking. Perhaps she'll never speak. We are safe.

The note wasn't signed, but the handwriting was familiar to me. Very familiar. I dropped the note. It fluttered to the floor. I flipped to the back of the ledger, to the doctor's notes, and glanced at the initials. Of course. S. F. That's why she was brought to St. Catherine's.

"What time is the first train out in the morning?" I asked Jonesy. He seemed surprised.

"Why?" asked MacCallum.

"Baltimore," I said. "We must go. We have to speak with Dr. Stanford Fuller. That was the last place I heard he was practicing. He has the answers."

Chapter 6

It was raining in Baltimore when we arrived. And by the time we stood on the doorstep, the doorstep that I remembered well, it was pouring. We were drenched. "Too bad that walking stick of yours isn't an umbrella," I said. MacCallum shrugged and smirked. I banged the knocker two more times against the door. At last, it opened. The woman who stood before me was young, perhaps in her twenties. "Hello," I said. "We're looking for Dr. Fuller."

The girl looked alarmed for a second. She looked away and down. "Just--just a moment," she said. She started to turn away and then stopped. "Oh," she said, as though just noticing the rain. "Won't you come in?"

We stood in the foyer, dripping, while we waited. A couple of minutes went by and then another woman appeared. This woman was older, much older. I didn't recognize her at first. Then I realized that this woman looked much older than the woman I had known previously. I tried to figure out just how long it had been since I had seen her. Three years? Four? She looked ten to twenty years older. Her face was drawn into a withered set of wrinkles, not all over, but certainly very much around the eyes and mouth. Her eyes sat within dark circles. She looked out warily. "Helen?" I said. She smiled briefly. It was only for an instant, however; a forced, friendly smile.

"John," she said simply. The smile came again and then left suddenly.

"Hello," I said. We've come to visit Stanford."

She gave a start when I spoke the words. A pained look spread across her face. "Come in," she said after a minute or so. "Clara," she hollered. "Please come collect these gentlemen's hats and coats."

The girl returned, full of apologies for not having taken them before. My guess is that we had startled her by asking for Dr. Fuller. And Mrs. Fuller was in a painful state, strained by our presence, or the fact that I had asked about Stanford. It wasn't too long before we found out why.

Mrs. Fuller invited us into the parlor. I was as familiar with it as I had been with the front stoop. I had visited them many times in the past, had eaten many a delightful meal with Stanford and Helen.

Once I had introduced her to MacCallum and she had made the offer of refreshments, which we respectfully declined, we sat. Mrs. Fuller sat across from us. She sighed and simply looked at me. She looked away for a second and then looked back.

"Perhaps we've come at a bad time," I started.

"No," she said. She sat quietly for another second, studying me with a very serious look. She sort of collapsed, at least in posture. "At this point," she said and hesitated again. "At this point, there would never be a good time."

"I'm sorry," I began. Both MacCallum and I started to rise.

"No, no," she said. "Please be seated. "All I meant was . . ."

She seemed at a loss, hesitating once more.

"Helen," I said. "What's wrong? What has happened? Has something happened to Stanford?"

"Yes," she said. "Most definitely--"

"I'm sorry, I--"

"Oh, no," she said. "Not what you're thinking. And it isn't so much what has happened to him. He has done it to himself. And . . . and I'm afraid there is no hope."

We sat looking at her. While MacCallum observed calmly, I was exasperated; I might even say astonished to some degree. I knew, or had heard that he had not been practicing the past couple of years, and there had been the rumors that alcohol might have been the reason. "I'm sorry," I said.

"Don't be," she started. Then she changed her stance after a second of thought. "We all are."

"I suppose I should . . ."

"Franklin!" She hollered. Then, rising from the chair, she went into the hall. "Franklin?" She turned to us again. "I'm sorry," she said. "It's just that I don't even know where to begin. I don't know how to describe it all. Having known him previously, you would not believe me if I told you. . . his condition."

"Yes, ma'am?" A man appeared, a servant.

"Franklin?" She hesitated and frowned for a second. It was no more than had she been pausing as though the thought of the rain, and asking him to go out into it might be too much to ask of him. "Franklin, could you please take these gentlemen to see Mr. Fuller?"

"I'm sorry, John, but this is the only way. Once you see him, his condition, you'll understand."

Franklin had simply nodded his response to her question. He went to retrieve his own hat and coat, while Helen asked Clara to retrieve ours.

In a few moments we were back out on the streets. We took a cab and pulled up near the docks. We followed Franklin quietly through the rain. The day was dark, and growing darker. The rain wasn't falling quite as hard as it had been, but was still coming down. Franklin stood before a door. He knocked. "Who is it?" someone hollered, a woman. Franklin just knocked again. After a couple of minutes the door opened a crack, an eye appeared, then a smile. "Well, hello, handsome!" She pulled the door wide then. A Creole prostitute, or so she appeared to be, stood before us. She was only half dressed. Her gown hung open. "He's a quiet one," she said. Glancing at us and smiling. She gave a wink. "I see you brought friends this time." She smiled ever wider, looking at Franklin. She was leaned against the doorjamb. Franklin stood immobile.

"Where is he?" Franklin asked.

The woman shrugged. "Try the usual places." She looked up, noting the rain. "My guess would be alley number two."

Franklin gave a nod and off we went again, MacCallum and I following like two lost puppies. "Come back when you can stay longer," the woman called behind us. Last glance I had she was still standing in the doorway grinning. Her arms were folded across her chest as she leaned against the jamb.

About five blocks away, we turned down a dark alley. There were a couple of bodies lying about. And another man sitting, leaning against the wall. He was staring straight ahead, as though there was something on the wall opposite him that required studying. Franklin looked around and then moved forward to where a tin overhang of sorts was supported by two two by fours. It hung down, not supported very well, and rainwater pattered on top of it and ran in runnels down and onto the body lying beneath it. That body was Stanford Fuller. He was oblivious to all of his surroundings. Franklin rolled him over. I squatted down and lifted his eyelids. He was alive, but in a drug induced state. Opium, I surmised. We just started to lift him, when there was a sound behind us. We turned. A large man stood grinning at the entrance to the alleyway. "Gents," he said. "I'll take over your wallets. Anything else of value."

I dropped Stanford's legs, leaving Franklin holding the upper half of Stanford's body. I stood. There was a quick flurry of movement beside me, MacCallum. The rapier had been unsheathed. He held it out before him, pointed at the man who had asked for our wallets. The man broke into uproarious laughter.

Being a doctor, I don't believe in the use of weapons. However, I am a practical man, and sometimes carrying a firearm is a deterrent of sorts. I had a revolver in my coat pocket. My fingers found it. I was just ready to pull it out.

"And just what do you intend to do with that?" the man asked. He roared again, almost doubling over laughing. MacCallum started to advance.

I pulled the gun out and pointed it. "I certainly know what I intend to do with this--"

"Now that's more like it," said the laughing man. "How're you doing Franklin?" He brushed past us, casually letting his coat slide open enough that we could see his badge. MacCallum and I exchanged glances. The large man stood looking down at Stanford. Franklin, still squatting, holding up the upper portion of the body, glanced up and nodded. "Gregson."

Gregson lifted his hat to readjust it. He had long, black, greasy bangs that fell forward across his forehead. Rainwater poured down and dripped from the bangs. He brushed them back with his left hand and reaffixed his hat. I shoved my gun into my pocket and went to help Franklin lift Stanford. "In a rough state, today," said Gregson. He didn't offer any assistance. Franklin grunted in agreement. We lifted. I realized within a minute that it didn't take both of us to lift Stanford. His body was so incredibly thin and light due to his wretched condition that it only took one man. And I had the distinct impression that Franklin had done this many times before. I stood back. Franklin tossed Stanford over his shoulder and started out of the alley. MacCallum and I followed. Gregson lifted his hat in a goodbye gesture. "Gents," he said.

Franklin barely got a knock on the door before it opened. The Creole woman had been expecting us.

Franklin and the woman worked to get Stanford out of his wet and dirty clothes. And I stood and watched, feeling useless. The two of them had him bundled and tucked into bed in mere minutes. It was a standardized routine, and the two had it down cold. I checked the pulse, and lifted the eyelids again. He was still alive, but he didn't have much longer. It might be a matter of days, or weeks, perhaps a month or two. In any case, the end was coming, not today, not from this venture, but soon. We all stood and looked. Once Stanford was settled and there was nothing more to be done, we all left. I saw Franklin slip some cash to the Creole woman before heading out the door. She smiled. "See you soon," she said. She looked beyond him, to where Mac-Callum and I stood waiting. "Y'all come back now, hear. Anytime, gentlemen." We just looked at her and she grinned. MacCallum nodded and I did the same.

"It's not what you think," said Franklin when we were back in the cab. "She looks after him as best she can. Mrs. Fuller pays her well to do it. No one can really help him at this point."

I had to concur with that. It was only a matter of waiting for the end.

"And Gregson?" said MacCallum. "Does he help look after him also?"

Franklin let out something between a chuckle and a snort. "Don't let the badge fool you. He's as dirty as they come." He paused for a second or so. "But he's well paid also."

I had the clear image then of Gregson rolling the other hapless bodies over in the alley and taking anything that might possibly be left, anything of any value. I even speculated on the possibility of him supplying the drugs, or at least taking a cut of the profits. I didn't ask. Stanford Fuller was my only concern. And like it or not, Stanford was on his way to a different world. He was already in a different world in a sense, or at least hanging on the edges of a shadowy fringe, a wraithlike existence. I knew not what thoughts lie within his mind now, but he would certainly be of no help to us with regard to the Children's Home.

***

Helen sighed. We had accepted coffee this time. "You see," she started. "Now, of course, why I couldn't explain."

"Yes," I responded. "Helen, I'm so sorry . . . but, I don't understand. He was a fine doctor, one of the best. And a good man."

She nodded. "He was." And then she corrected herself. "He is. He is a good man, still. Or at least that's what I keep telling myself. I've long ceased to visit. It's been several months now. I just can't . . . I struggle with it on a daily basis, but I just can't. I finally had to accept the fact that it was the end, that there was nothing I could do. Once he passes, then I'll see him. I dread that day, even. I try not to dwell on what he will look like then, what condition the body will be in, how ravaged and wasted it—he . . ."

I thought for a second that she was going to break. She came close. She paused and one or two tears started. She sniffled. Then she stopped. She was a strong woman.

"But what was the cause?" I asked.

She shook her head.

"But there had to be something, some initial cause. Something had to have happened for him to break." I waited. She waited.

And then she spoke. "First he started drinking heavily . . ."

"Yes, but that wouldn't have . . ."

"No," she said. "There was something else. I don't know what, but there was something behind it. A cause. He would never say. I tried, John. I tried to find out. I questioned him. He would never say. He only got angry when I continued to ask. I stopped. And then he started . . ."

I waited. Again, she started to break. Again, she caught herself. She held steady.

"All I could figure out was that whatever it was had happened, happened before we came here. It must have had something to do with his time at St. Catherines."

"Did he keep a diary?" asked MacCallum. Any sort of journal? Anything regarding his work? Research papers? Anything?"

I gave him a disparaging look. He shouldn't be drilling her with questions like that. It was—

"No, she said. No journal, at least not that I'm aware of. My husband wasn't an introspective man, Mr. MacCallum. Not really. John, you knew him as well as anyone . . ."

"No," I said. "He wasn't—isn't the introspective type at all." She glanced at me, seemingly caught off guard by my changing to the present tense. He wasn't dead, after all. A faint, hint of a sad smile touched her lips. She even seemed pleased for a second, that I would still allow that respect. Her and I had both veered back and forth across the line between what he had been and what he had become. I realized then that she had resigned herself to his current state, to his death. And I realized too, as I had back at the Creole woman's place, that he wasn't the same man that he had been. I conceded. The past tense was the only way to refer to the man, Stanford, the outstanding doctor that I had known. The man that I had considered a friend, that I had once known, that man was long gone.

Chapter 7

"It's a shame we couldn't find anything," said MacCallum.

We were on our way back to Riverton. We had caught the last train. I sat silent. Helen had kindly allowed us to look through all of Stanford's papers. We went through his office, looking for anything that might help. It all was so unseemly to me. Even with Helen's consent, I felt disgusted. And there had been nothing. It had all been a wild goose chase. But something had happened to Stanford Fuller. There had been a sea-change, at some point. Since it appeared to have happened while he was at St. Catherines, then that was where we would have to look. But how? Where? We couldn't just go barging in, looking through paperwork. What paperwork would we look through? What would we even look for? Did it all have something to do with the girl, Alice? Or could it have been something totally different? There had been many, many patients, any one of which could have been the catalyst. Or none of them. Anything could have happened to him, at any point. His condition, his downfall, could have been triggered by something totally unrelated. And then a thought crept into my mind. The note. The words . . .

The girl is still traumatized. She isn't speaking. Perhaps she'll never speak. We are safe.

Those words had, in fact, been written in the hand of Stanford Fuller. And those words, most definitely, referred to Alice.

***

Jonesy was waiting for us when we arrived at the station. He was beaming. "It worked," he said. "Mrs. Rowland intervened. You've got the rest of the week."

It was Wednesday now, evening. But that gave us three days. And that was a little . . . "It isn't enough time, but it--"

"Nonsense," we'll have it all worked out by tomorrow evening.

"What?" I asked. Incredulous. I looked at Jonesy. He was grinning even wider, but he also had a surprised look on his face. "But we have nothing," I said. "It's madness to think we can get to the bottom of this in that length of time. No Alice to talk to. Father Andreas is dead. Stanford Fuller is also, well . . . We've got nothing."

"Not true," said MacCallum. He turned to Jonesy. "Jonesy, can you bring all of the photos from the file box. Every one you can find that shows the children hanging."

Jonesy grinned. "I can bring the whole box, if you want."

"If you want," said MacCallum. "But the photos should be enough."

"Sure thing," Jonesy said. He started to turn away.

"Jonesy," MacCallum said. Jonesy turned back with a questioning look.

"How did Sheriff Carroll take the intrusion of the widow Rowland?"

Jonesy grinned his usual wide open, friendly grin. "He didn't like it a bit."

"I thought he might not."

"But he knew better than to go up against her. One word from her and the townsfolk would run him out of office. Besides, he does still have enough respect for her deceased husband." He paused for a minute, still grinning. "But he still didn't like it."

MacCallum smiled.

***

"I still don't understand," I said. We were back in the hotel room now. I was completely perplexed. We did have the note, the one in Stanford's hand. And it had been tucked away in Father Andreas's notebook. So, one could make the assumption that the two of them were the guilty parties. But still it made no sense. Neither of them would have had any reason to hang all the children . . . none that I could imagine, at least. And to say that the whole thing was almost solved seemed, to my mind, preposterous. "We have nothing," I said. "We can go back to

St. Catherine's and slip into the basement to search out the girl's file, but . . . that's it. It's the only path open. It's all we've got."

MacCallum stood, grinning. "Benson," he said. "I'm surprised at you. One night of burglary, and suddenly the rules are out the window. Next thing we know, you'll be rolling opium addicts in the alley like our friend—what was the man's name?"

"Oh, shut up," I said. "Gregson, that was his name. And he had a badge. He could get away with a lot more than I possibly could. Now, what the devil do you have up your sleeve? Spill it."

He laughed. "I'll show you all the cards, which would be all I've got up my sleeve. Nothing liquid, I assure you--"

"Phew," I said. I was starting to get hot under the collar. "Now you're just being--"

"Relax, I'll fill you in when Jonesy gets here with the photos. What time have you got?"

I pulled out my pocket watch. "Ten past seven."

"Good, the night's still young enough. It might all end to--" A knock sounded on the door. "That's either Jonesy, or our friend Peter."

"You still think Peter purloined important sections of Andreas's book?'

"I won't know how important until we see them. I do know he's eaten up with guilt. He can't wait to get those pages to us. He won't be able to stand it for much longer." The knock sounded again. Mac-Callum opened the door. It was Jonesy. He had just started to set the box down and give the door another loud whack, or try the knob, when it was opened. He entered and set the box on the bed.

"I brought the whole thing, just in case."

"That's fine," said MacCallum.

Jonesy fished through the box and pulled out three photos, while MacCallum opened his small case and brought out his magnifying glass. We all moved over to the table where the lantern was. Jonesy and I sat in the chairs while MacCallum laid out the photos. Two of the photos appeared identical. Both showed the children hanging. The photo was taken from an angle. It was not taken of the children from the front. Perhaps that would have been too grim, but in any case, . . .

"Remember when I said that something was bothering me?"

I nodded. Jonesy looked on with interest. Now take the glass and look closely, right here." He had looked first, to pinpoint what he was talking about.

"Now," he said. Count the children. How many do you see?"

"Well," I said. "Eight, . . . the seven hanging, and if you count the girl who fell, Alice, eight."

I passed the glass across to Jonesy. "I concur," he said. He shrugged. MacCallum's eyebrows were raised slightly, seemingly in dismay at something we were missing. "Didn't even need the glass to see," said Jonesy. "We could count them easily enough without it."

"True," said MacCallum. "However, in order to count the nooses . . ." He placed the other photo so we could see it. It was a photo of the ropes, after the children had been cut down. There was the long strand, on the end, presumably where Alice had been. It had been the longest bit of rope hanging, where it had frayed and unfurled. It hadn't needed cutting, because there had been no body dangling. The other lengths had been cut. They had been cut closer up toward the branch that they had been tied to. One could imagine, someone holding the bodies up, one at a time, while someone else cut the rope. And it would have been easier cutting close to the tree branch, since each body would have, being held from below, caused the rope to go slack. Of course,

117

the body would have been held to keep it from dangling and swinging while the person cut the rope. It simply would have been too difficult, and horrid . . .

"Now look," said MacCallum. "Only, this time, count the lengths of hanging rope. Now that the children are out of the photo. They have all been cut down. Do you see?"

Jonesy looked. He still had the glass. He didn't even have to hold it close. "Holy Jesus," he said. "How could we have missed it? There are nine pieces of rope hanging." He handed the glass and the photo over to me.

There was the long one, closest to the tree trunk, which hadn't needed cutting, and then a short one, and then another sort of longish one, . . . and then six more very short pieces all cut close up to the branch. Sure enough, there were nine total. I pulled the photo with the children hanging. I looked. The second one away from the tree trunk, the first body, actually, blocked the view. The ropes appeared as one, almost. You had to look really close; But, if you moved your eyes up the rope, leading up from the boy, and then looked down the branch, you could see it. Not very clearly, however, and you had to be specifically looking for it. I looked back at the photo with just the ropes dangling, the photo taken head-on, and it was obvious—there were nine ropes.

"Good God."

"Yes, but I wonder . . ."

"I know," I said. "How good a God could he be to let these beautiful young children be so ruthlessly hanged."

"No," said MacCallum. "That's not what I meant. Do you still have the other photo?"

"What other photo?" asked Jonesy.

"The other one of just the ropes."

"There isn't one. This is all there is."

"There was another photo," said MacCallum. "Wait," he said. He went to his valise and flipped it open. There was a folded newspaper. He brought it over. It wasn't the local Gazette, however. But there were two photos. The prominent one was of the hanging children, and then below it, the one with just the ropes. There were only eight rope pieces in this one. One had been removed.

Jonesy whistled through his teeth, just a short, pushing out of his breath. It was a haunting sound.

"But wait," I said. "Anything could have happened between one photo being taken and another."

"True," said MacCallum. "Who took the photos?"

"Why, Bill Short, he takes all our . . . What?"

MacCallum and I both were grinning at him. We had the same thought. "You mean, there is something around here that you don't do?" I asked.

Jonesy smirked. "Anyways, that photo is from another paper, a neighboring town. So someone was up and had started cutting the ropes off the branch maybe, and the photographer interrupted whoever it was so he could take a photo of just the ropes."

"And the person could have started cutting the ropes off randomly." I knew what MacCallum was thinking, and I tried to head him off. In his mind, things weren't random. Doubt started to creep into my mind, right after I said it. It was possible, of course. . .

"Possibly," MacCallum conceded. "But we need to find out who cut the ropes down. I suspect I know who it was, and possibly why."

Chapter 8

I was growing impatient. MacCallum had left with Jonesy, and I was to await Jonesy's return. I'm not one to sit idle. Oh, sure, I can relax well enough on train and carriage rides, doze even. But when I'm waiting on someone, it is a whole different thing altogether. I lasted about ten minutes. I grabbed my hat and coat and headed down to the lobby. That's where I ran into Peter. He bumped right into me. He had his head down, deep in thought, and I had just pulled my watch out of its pocket to check the time. Good thing the watch was on a chain. We both, of course, were startled. "Oh, I'm sorry," I said. That's when I saw the tormented and frightened face of young Peter. He looked up at me, his eyes wide with fear and anguish.

"I—I—I'm sorry. I--"

"Yes, yes, I know, you're here to give us the missing pages . . ."

"Y—yes, but how? How did you know?"

He dug into his cassock and pulled out the bunch of them. I was surprised at the bulk of the pages. There were more than I had expected. "Here," he said. He handed me something more, another page or two. He was hesitant. And he then stood shuffling his feet, or I at least assumed they were shuffling somewhere in the folds of the cloth that extended to the floor almost. He was unsure of what to do next.

"You're doing the right thing, son," I said. I tried to sound fatherly. I'm not sure he bought into it. But it didn't matter right then, because Jonesy appeared.

"You ready?" Jonesy asked me. Then he looked at Peter and nodded. Peter hesitantly nodded back.

"Let's go," I said. And off we started. I stopped. Peter still stood there, his mouth hanging open. I don't know whether he thought I was going to invite him up to the room so he could explain more about the papers, but there wasn't time. Perhaps I would have. It could have been informative, but the plan was set in motion, and there was a certain time element involved. "Father Andreas would be proud of you," I said. I couldn't possibly know if I spoke the truth, never having laid eyes on Father Andreas while he had been alive. I never knew the man. I'm sure it didn't matter. Peter undoubtedly felt a little more comfortable for my having said it. I could see it in his face. With that, we left.

***

When we got to the stable, Mr. Farrow wasn't there. The stable boy was the only one. "Hi, Tommy," said Jonesy. "We need a carriage. Well, he does, I mean." I figured, due to the lateness of the hour, Jonesy lent me more credibility.

The boy looked puzzled at first, and then curious. "Oh, sure," he said. "Coming right up." He waited just a bit before asking. "Where you headed?" Jonesy and I looked at one another, a little surprised. The boy's shiner was just healing up nicely.

"Oh, just out to the Monastery," said Jonesy. Mr. Benson, here, needs to talk to that young monk, ah, what's his name . . .?"

"Peter," I said helpfully.

"Oh," said Tommy. No need to ride out. I just saw him. He's in town.

"Oh, really?"

"Yeah. Just spotted him a few minutes ago."

"Oh, well. We were supposed to meet up with Father Bartholomew, also," I volunteered.

"Oh, okay. I didn't see him." He smiled. He cheerfully hooked up the horse.

Just before climbing into the carriage, I turned and spoke to Jonesy. "Perhaps we should see if young Peter needs a lift back home?"

"Maybe. He just might."

We climbed in and then slowly rode away. Half mile out of town, I turned to Jonesy and grinned. "You think he bought it?"

"He'll beat us there; you can count on it."

***

All was darkness when we arrived at the Children's home. The moon had risen, but the cloud cover kept its light from extending down on the grounds. There was a certain quiet. It was too quiet. Nothing was stirring just yet, but that was all about to change. Jonesy and I climbed down from the carriage. I carried the lantern and we moved toward the front steps. We were careful to mind where the broken step was, and stepped around and over the hole. The next step up creaked. The sound was loud and however short, hung in the quietness. We pushed the door open; The divan hadn't been moved back to its obstructive position. Everything seemed the same. The box off to the left, and the jar of liquid, both sat undisturbed. Even the rocker sat quiet. The silence was deafening. My imagination wanted to bring forth the laughing and playing children, but I was stern and made sure they all stayed tucked in tight, all fast asleep. No need for them to be underfoot. Not tonight. I turned to Jonesy. "Now what?"

"Now we wait."

We walked toward the bed with the dangling ropes and the sheet hanging down onto the floor, just the corner of it, undisturbed. The ropes put me in mind of the pieces hanging from the branch in the photos. Nine, and then eight. I crouched and waited. Jonesy took the lantern and went into the front room. He didn't go all the way to the front, but stood leaning against the banister. He needed to be close enough.

He talked, saying his lines, just as though I was right there listening. After a few minutes of nothing happening, except my knees reminding me that I was getting up in age, I sat. I sat just for a minute, just to give my knees a rest. It was just a few more seconds before the trapdoor lifted. I could sense it more than hear it, but it lifted all the same. It did give a slight sound, though I wouldn't call that sound a creak. I waited a second or so, and then slammed my fist hard against it. Shiner number two, I thought. You think he would have learned after the first time. There was a sound of him tumbling and a squeal-like grunt. I don't know how far the drop was, but it wouldn't much matter. The surprise factor played into it, causing the drop to seem steep, I'm sure. I rose to my feet and went out to the doorway of the room. "The mouse is in the trap," I said. "Let's hope the escape has been cut off." It wasn't long after that we heard the loud commotion of MacCallum and the young lad coming around the side of the house. We went to the front door. Mac-Callum had the boy by the scruff of the shirt neck. Tommy Mifflin apparently hadn't used the front entrance since I had fallen through the step. He stepped right into the hole and tripped. The boy was going to have quite a few bruises in the morning. MacCallum lifted him up and nudged him in through the door. The lad was cursing like a sailor. He couldn't have been any more than sixteen, just a couple of years older than young Alice. I had obviously seen him at the stable, but hadn't had the chance to observe him as closely as I had now. He was rather scrawny, wiry. He had to be to fit in the tunnel I supposed. Though he didn't look small enough that he could fit through the trapdoor. Perhaps that's why he only lifted it to observe. He came and went through the outer entrance of the tunnel. Had I been able to reach under the bed and grab him, there would have been no way to bring him up through the hole. It would have been a standoff. No one would have been able to go in either direction. MacCallum would not have been able to fit in the narrow tunnel. It might have been wider at the entrance, however.

"So where is it, the outer entrance?"

"Under the wagon," said MacCallum. "Perfectly disguised. But he led me straight to it. All I had to do was wait in the darkness for him to show. Good job of luring him here, by the way."

The boy scowled from where he sat on the floor. "I just wanted to see what the two of you were up to." He looked at Jonesy and then me.

"We know that you were here the morning of the hanging," said MacCallum. He waited a second or so. "You were up in the tree with them."

There was a distinct look of surprise that sprung up in the kid's eyes. "I wasn't. I wasn't here."

We all stood waiting. I expected MacCallum to say something else. I believe he started to, but didn't get the chance.

The kid spoke again. "I only climbed up afterwards, to cut all the rope down from the tree."

I caught MacCallum's eye, his smirk. Jonesy was grinning too. Tommy had, of course, just volunteered information that had only been suspected. We wouldn't have been able to find out until we asked the photographer the next day. And the photographer might not have even remembered.

MacCallum took it a step further. "And you were in the tree at the time of the hanging. Perhaps you also had a noose around your neck." He waited. Tommy sat silent, staring at the floor now. He was a little less angry, and a little more scared. Not a lot. Too much time had gone by. But the time was lessening in his mind, apparently. It was written on his face. He was taking a trip back through time. His mind was reeling, perhaps. His breathing became shorter. I'm quite sure his heart started to beat a little faster. Soon enough he was back—

There was a commotion outside. "Watch your step," someone said. The front door, which I believe MacCallum had closed after shoving the boy inside. I wouldn't swear to having seen him do it. But it opened now. And in walked—"Ms. Ephram?" And she had Alice in tow. Alice wore the black eye patch. The scar ran down the side of her face, a deep runnel. Her head, of course, was tilted to the side. She was terrified. Her good eye was ripe with horror. She looked down at Tommy. She started trembling. She stopped herself from doing so, or at least brought it down a notch, by looking away. She looked down at the floor. Still shivering.

"But what?" I asked. I was shocked. I couldn't believe Ms. Ephram would bring her here. The setback would be tremendous. I was sure the girl would never recover now. I was quite sure that she would be whisked back to the tragedy. She would experience it again, just as Tommy was re-experiencing that morning, just now, as they had stepped up on

129

the porch. "But why?" I looked at Ms. Ephram. My mind reeled. It had been obvious to me how traumatized the girl had been when MacCallum and I had stopped by with the intent to question her. There had been no doubt how terrified she had been then. Not of MacCallum, of course, but of me, just seeing me. That alone had transported her back to St. Catherine's, and then, I am sure, back to the morning of the hanging. It must have been awful for her. And Ms. Ephram had been extremely upset. "But why? Ms. Ephram, why? How could you bring her here? Here, of all places."

"Yes, Dr. Benson. Yes, I know. I know. I know, of course that under normal circumstances . . . under normal circumstances. I would never."

It was as though her and I were transported back to the hospital, back to the time of, well, back when Alice was a resident. Back when Alice was a five-year old little girl, unable to speak of the horror. It was as though I was lecturing Ms. Ephram on some, some clerical error she had made on a record, or something of the like. Surely, surely, I wouldn't have to give her any lecture, or advice about bringing the girl back here. It should simply never happen. Ms. Ephram knew it should never happen. She knew—of course she knew—not to bring the girl here, to the sight of the shock. Oh my God, I thought. My God, woman, what have you done? I had to say no more. She knew my thoughts. Of course, she certainly knew my thoughts. She looked away, and then down at the floor, just as Alice had done. All of us stood in silence. We all waited. For what I don't know. . . something. I looked up from Ms. Ephram. I looked over her shoulder. "Robert?" It was Robert Fuller. I didn't understand. What was he? What was he doing here? And there was someone else. And that someone was the Deputy, the local Deputy, what was his name? My head was spinning. It all seemed like a nightmare. I kept coming back to Ms. Ephram bringing Alice here. Why?

The Deputy spoke. "Tommy? Tommy, what are you doing here? What's going on?" He had come in last, and hadn't seen his brother right away. The lantern sat on the stairway, just where Jonesy had left it. The light was strange coming up from below. Everyone's face was lit from lower than the natural way of things. It all seemed like a comedy of errors, with everyone showing up, and everyone looking for answers. "Answer me," said the Deputy. "What are you doing?"

131

"He was just going to tell us about the morning of the ha--" MacCallum stopped, wisely I thought, right in mid-sentence. The deputy moved into the room now, going over to MacCallum.

"What?" Asked the Deputy. "What was he going to say?"

"He was going to confess."

The Deputy looked shocked. His mouth hung open. He was angry. He was going to speak. Words came, but not his. It was Ms. Ephram who was speaking. She spoke in a monotone voice, still looking at the floor. It was as though nothing had transpired since I had asked why she had brought Alice here. And she felt the need to respond, apparently, with some sort of answer. "After you left the other morning . . . after the two of you left, Alice was hysterical." She mechanically reached up and placed her hand on the girl's shoulder. Alice continued looking at the floor. And Ms. Ephram was still looking at the floor. "But she calmed. After an hour or so, she calmed down. She spoke. For the first time, she spoke of the morning. She relayed it in great detail." There was a sense of panic in the room. Several of the crowd became tense and nervous. Tommy looked up with a special fear. But hadn't he just been about to confess?

. . . "She was very calm then." I looked at the girl. She, in fact, seemed calm now, much calmer and more in control than she had been just moments earlier. "And then, well, . . . then she said that Tommy needed her, that he was in trouble." Everyone looked at Tommy. He looked up, a partial scowl still on his face.

"Not that Tommy," said Alice.

"No," Ms. Ephram said. "Her voice was strange, her faint smile rode along her voice, as though there was some stringed instrument that was strumming out her voice, just the one word, No. It was a hauntingly strange voice, an elongated sound. She smiled down at Alice. But Alice wasn't looking at her. Three more words played out on the instrument. "Not that Tommy." The air quivered with a nervous energy, a hum.

"That Tommy," said Alice. Her voice was extremely calm. The rocking chair rocked slowly. That was where Alice pointed. All eyes moved to look at it. The light was coming up from that weird, unnatural angle, lighting all of our faces. The rocking chair rocked. "Tommy the mouse," There was almost a joy in her voice. It wasn't like the plucked string of a second ago, not like Ms. Ephram's voice. It was a happy voice though. Alice was happy, at least in that moment.

MacCallum was the only one of us who acted. He ran around behind the chair and stomped his foot down. I knew what he was doing, or at least trying to do. And so did the Tommy who was still sitting on the floor—Tommy, the would be confessor. But just as MacCallum stomped his foot down, which did nothing to stop the rocker from rocking, some-thing happened. There was a—and this is the only way I know how to describe it—a swirl, a swirl of mist or smoke, or call it what you will. It moved, sped over to Alice, to her side. She leaned down. "Tommy's afraid," she said. "He thinks you're going to hurt him again. Just like before." She looked up. She pointed at the Deputy. "You killed the soldier. You and the others. And then you killed Tommy. Tommy the mouse. He didn't stand a chance." Dep-uty Daniel Mifflin looked stunned, stunned and frightened. His secret was out.

"That's right," said Jonesy. I had forgotten about him. He had been standing quietly, taking it all in, the whole of the comedy—or tragedy, all of the absurdity. "You would have been here then, during that time. You were."

"I—I, this is crazy talk. Nonsense. I had nothing to do with it . . ."

"You did," said Alice. She was calm and composed. She looked at him with her cocked head and her one good eye. She continued on with details of how the soldier was tortured. She said that the man's bones are still embedded in the wall of the tunnel beneath the house, some of them sticking out, just enough to see. She looked at Tommy on the floor. "Tell them Tommy. Tell them about the bones . . ."

Tommy had a frightened look, but then he nodded. "They're there," he mumbled.

"And Tommy," continued Alice. She turned stiffly in his direction. "Are you going to tell them about that morning, that morning in the tree? Tell them about Charlie, Tommy. Tell them about little Charlie, Tommy. Tell them how he cried. I saw him cry. He was scared. He didn't want to fly. His foot slipped and he was scared. I tried to calm him. I tried to help him. I couldn't do it out loud though. I tried to calm him with my mind. I smiled at him. But he was scared. His foot slipped. The branch was wet and he slipped. You said that we could all fly,

Tommy. You said the rope would protect us. It would hold us if it didn't work. You said that, Tommy. You stood there on the other side of Charlie. You were angry. You commanded him to do it. Just like you told all of us to do it. You had the rope on your neck too, Tommy, but you took yours off. You didn't fly, Tommy. You were scared. But I flew, didn't I? I was the only one. It hurt, Tommy. I was scared too. It--"

No one had seen the deputy pull out his gun. All eyes had been on the girl. Alice. All faces, in the eerie light from below. All faces, all eyes were on Alice. No one even knew what the loud noise was, the loud bang. Not at first.

There was a commotion, just after the shot was fired. It took me a second to realize. I felt a smile spread across my face. MacCallum's walking stick had come sharply down on the Deputy's arm. The gun dropped and skittered across the floor. I thought all was well. I thought MacCallum had knocked the gun away in good time, and that the shot had gone harmlessly astray. MacCallum was on top of him then. Jonesy went quickly, to assist, to hold the Deputy pinned to the floor. I stood stupidly, and watched. It must have been the light. The

136

weird light. It was affecting me, all of us. I looked over. Alice had slumped down. We all looked. Blood had started coming out of the hole in the front of Alice's dress. Her dress was becoming soaked. Blood dripped from her mouth. I could see it. It fell in drops, large drops, onto the floor. But then she raised up, and the blood was slowly being sucked back into her mouth. It was strange. I looked at Ms. Ephram, who was still standing next to Alice. She too was watching it, seeing it all. Alice stood up again, slowly. The blood on her dress slid up and back into her. The hole closed. The bullet hole simply closed up. It appeared that everything was moving in reverse. Alice raised up. The swirling cloud, or whatever it was, Tommy, Tommy the mouse, was healing her, or doing something of the like. Whatever he was doing, he was taking away her pain, removing the cause of it. The bullet hole closed right up. And something else was happening. Her neck straightened. She stood up straight. And in that strange light, that very night. I saw it. And Ms. Ephram saw it. She watched; her mouth open. We watched. The runnel disappeared. It slipped up Alice's face and beneath the eye patch. The eye patch stayed in place. It didn't move. The girl then collapsed. I tried to get there, but Ms. Ephram managed. Just as Alice was at the floor, Ms. Ephram's hand, her arm, slid beneath the girl's body. We lifted her, Ms. Ephram and I, and carried her in to the bed, the one above the trap door, the bed with the dangling ropes. I lifted the sheet and shook the rat feces off of it. We laid the girl down.

I heard someone talking in the front room. I returned to it. It was Tommy speaking. MacCallum was standing over him. The boy was sitting on the floor still. He was telling about the morning. He was telling pretty much the same story that Alice had told. But his story had a different twist. "It was the drugs," he said. "The mushrooms. I used to go with the priest in the morning sometimes. He taught me about them. He had shared his knowledge with the doctor, Doctor Fuller. They used to discuss them, the mushrooms, I mean. And other drugs, the effects. They used to discuss the merits. Then came the experiments. I would grind the mushrooms up, the particular kind, the ones that the priest had taught me about. I would put some of what I had made in all of the kid's food. At first, they got sick. Each one would act strangely. Each in his or her own way. But then, after a time, they stopped being sick. They became calm. And then the suggestions started. The doctor told me how to do it, what to say. . ."

"That's a lie." This time it was Robert Fuller speaking. He had been quiet until now. He had simply been an observer. But now it all touched on his older brother, Stanford. The whole picture was becoming clear now. "That's a lie," he said again. "The boy's lying. My brother would never do such a thing. Ever."

I had my hand on my revolver then. It was in my coat pocket, but it was ready. I was ready. No one else would be shot. And I doubted that Tommy the mouse would come to anyone else's rescue if they were. Robert did start toward the boy. He started to lunge. All it took was for me to speak. "Robert," I said. He stopped and looked at me.

"But you knew him," he said to me. "You know he wouldn't do such a thing. . ."

"And I just saw him this morning," I said. My God, had it only just been this morning. I wanted to look at my watch. I didn't. The night was starting to fade, slowly. It was moving into morning. I left it at that. That had been enough. Robert knew that if I had seen his brother, then I knew that something had

happened. Something had changed him. That something could easily have been the hangings of that
morning. It could have been Alice. I certainly now
believed that that in fact *was* it. I thought of the
note. The words came to me again. He must have
felt guilty. He was.

 I needed to hear no more of what the boy had to
say. I went in to tend to Alice. Ms. Ephram lay beside her on the bed. Alice was dead. The grayness of
the dawn was upon us then, no more craziness of
the light coming at weird angles from a lantern on
the lower step of the stairs.

 I'll shorten the rest of the story. I have to confess
that I lost interest after Alice died. Right then and
there, that very morning. I had only been interested
in the hanging, finding out the truth about what had
happened that morning, how the children came to
be hanged. I can see them, dangling in the dawn. It
still haunts me, sometimes.

 And the rest, those who were guilty, well, I'm not
sure exactly what happened with the two brothers. I
know there was a trial of sorts for each of them . . . I
didn't follow it. To my mind, no punishment would
have been harsh enough. I try to think fairly of all
men, but to harm innocent little children . . .

Stanford passed on a couple of weeks later. I didn't attend the funeral. I don't think Helen really expected me to, even though she sent word.

And Father Andreas, well, I handed over the papers that Peter had given me to MacCallum. They were, in fact, a confession. He too, felt guilty. And though it is a mortal sin for a priest, monk, or even a layperson, or follower of the faith to commit suicide, Father Andreas felt that he deserved it for what he had done. I believe that within the confession he stated that he left it up to God, himself, to decide. Whether he deserved to remain in hell or not. It is odd, but the Sheriff had that part right all along.

And as for Peter, well, he turned into quite a mature and interesting fellow. He takes his walks after morning-prayer. I see him sometimes. It has been several years on since that night and morning of Alice's death. I have retired and now own the place, The Children's home. It is still called that. And why not? It is full of orphaned children. Ms. Ephram— Rita, and I, take care of them. We cleaned up the place, got it back into shape. All of the children who were hanged that morning are buried in the small cemetery that is behind the house, just a short-ways from the garden. Little Charlie, scared little Charlie.

And Tommy the mouse is there, and even Alice. We pulled the eye patch off that morning that she died. All was healed. Her eyes looked the same. Both were a beautiful blue. Well, one was a little bit lighter shade, but not by much. Both eyes were in tact. Her neck was straightened. She had flown, I thought. She was the only one.

And so now there is laughter. Not only is the place cleaned and painted, and fully operational, but the tunnel has been filled in with dirt. The soldier is properly buried. In the evenings, late in the summer, after dinner, when Rita and I are sitting on the front porch and watching the children play, well, those are the happiest of times. The children laugh and run around trying to catch fireflies, and sometimes ladybugs, even a dragonfly, or grasshopper, etc. And often, a small child will climb up onto my lap and tell me he (or she) has just seen Alice, and a little boy they say is called Tommy the mouse. They say they mostly see them playing and lingering around the garden, which is kind of close to the small cemetery. "Really?" I laugh. "You don't say?" And the child giggles. I looked over at Rita, to see if she had heard. She simply smiles.

Oh, and my old friend MacCallum? I still get a letter from him now and again. I think he is about to propose to Miss Victoria, or whatever her name was. Not sure if he ever became intrigued with anymore cases. As is the case with myself, I think this one was the only one.

I don't know when MacCallum's wedding will be, but Robert Fuller is due to wed Rita's niece, Emily. Apparently, that was who she was off to meet the morning MacCallum and I stopped by the Ephram household. I thought it odd, that night. And I'll admit to being extremely suspicious as to why Robert Fuller had shown that night. I had assumed he had been there to protect his brother's reputation, to hide or obfuscate the facts. But it turned out to be simply a case of him volunteering to escort Rita and Alice. And Deputy Mifflin was the escort for all of them. He hadn't expected his little brother to be there, or any of the rest of us. And he was certainly surprised by Tommy the mouse and Alice spilling his secret.

In any case, Robert was along in case the girl needed medical attention. She did, in fact, and we all failed her. That night, all of us failed Alice. Tommy the mouse was the only one who looked after her, tried to protect her. And maybe in his own way, he did. He brought her safely to the other side. He made her whole, before helping her over. I'm sure little Charlie is there too. The children don't mention seeing him, but perhaps he's just too shy to show himself. Maybe one day . . .

And, oh yeah, Jonesy. I can't forget our friendly man of all trades. He comes by once every two weeks or so to join in a game of whist. The evenings he doesn't show, the children, along with Rita and myself have a good bit of fun playing croquet. There is generally a large, raucous sound of laughter in the air; Just as there should be in a Children's home.

Note to reader:

First regarding the dedication to Genie. I had to move the full dedication to the end of the book, because it became so intense. I didn't want to spoil any fun and entertainment that you might get out of this book.

Dedicated to Genie (not her real name), and to all the Genies of the world.

And, totally unrelated to Genie, to any and every child I got to visit and work with in Morocco (mostly we just sang *Wheels on the Bus*). I might as well expand the thought to include every child the world over. No child should have to suffer any sort of horror whatsoever, whether it be war, famine, abuse, or anything else horrific the world throws at them.

This is a fictional work of history, imaginary "fun detective/horror," and totally unrelated to Genie, and what she went through.

To find out more about Genie, read the Russ Rymer book of the same name. It is a tragic and heartbreaking story. I didn't start out thinking of her when I started this book; but for generally obvious reasons (or what will become obvious reasons if you read the Rymer book), Genie popped into my mind at some point, and the thought of her wouldn't leave. No child should ever have to suffer what she went through. And yet, her beautiful spirit showed through, as related in that book. The sad fact is that the Russ Rymer book was a true account, and not a tale of fiction. While Genie's circumstances were totally different from the children in this book, she popped into my mind. It was the character, Alice, who brought Genie to mind, I guess. She wasn't modelled on Genie, of course; but hints, then thoughts of Genie rose up, well after Alice took shape. The only real connection was that each became warped, or affected, by incidents of tragedy in childhood.

***

Thank you very much for reading. I mean this sincerely. I love sharing. If you enjoyed this story then please leave a review on Amazon. I cannot tell you how much it helps me.

Also, if you enjoyed this book, then be sure and check out my other titles:

The Dancing Man (a rollicking, rockin' horror novella)

Esmirana's Trunk: Tales of Mystery and Suspense!

The Soft Eloquence of Neon (a collection of early short stories)

The Civil War Dark Tales series (horror/ghost tales):
Volume one: Daguerreotype Dreams
Volume two: I Fear Only the Dogs
Volume three: And You Shall Not Live!
Volume four: The Scarecrow.

Science Fiction:
The Red Kimono (a collection of Sci-fi stories).

Nonfiction:
Write Play Love: How I Write Short Stories

Format Your Book: How to Format Your Manuscript for Amazon using MS Word!

And very soon to be released fiction:

Pirate Tales: Cap'n's Eyes
And other eerie stories

Again, Thank You, Thank You, Thank You
for reading.

You can catch me on Goodreads (one of my favorite
hangouts), or visit my website at
www.markstattelman.com

Thank You again!

Mark Stattelman